AN ACCIDENTAL SHROUD

AN ACCIDENTAL SHROUD

Marjorie Eccles

St. Martin's Press ⋒ New York

A THOMAS DUNNE BOOK.
An imprint of St. Martin's Press.

AN ACCIDENTAL SHROUD.

Library of Congress Cataloging-in-Publication Data

Eccles, Marjorie.
    An accidental shroud : an Inspector Mayo
mystery / by Marjorie Eccles.
        p.   cm.
    "A Thomas Dunne book."
    ISBN 0-312-15045-8
    1. Mayo, Gil (Fictitious character)—Fiction.
2. Police—England—Fiction.   I. Title.
PR6055.C33A64   1997
823'.914—dc20   96-32948
                                 CIP

First published in Great Britain by Collins Crime,
an imprint of HarperCollins*Publishers*

First U.S. Edition: January 1997

10   9   8   7   6   5   4   3   2   1

ACKNOWLEDGEMENTS

My thanks are due to Gary Cox, to Ian Harris of
N. Bloom & Son (Antiques) Ltd, and to
Geoffrey Munn and his staff at Wartski, for their
very generous help and advice

PROLOGUE

October

He was beginning to wish he'd picked a better night for the murder, but it was too late for that now, though the storm was growing worse. Then he saw how it might work to his advantage, and his mood lifted.

The weathermen had forecast winds of epic proportions, and for once they'd been right. He'd never experienced anything like it; he imagined this was how the Blitz must have been, with the din of bombs and flying debris and the exhilarating smell of danger. The thought of death and destruction excited him. It was the sort of night when chimney-stacks blew down and people were killed by falling trees and flying roof tiles, but it was providing him with perfect cover. Nobody in their right mind would be out who didn't absolutely have to.

Their right mind! He nearly laughed at that.

He knew that anyone making a calculated decision to kill, as he had done, would be thought evil, or mad, but he wasn't mad, and he didn't feel evil: cool and clever was what he felt. Cool and clever and high on his own cleverness and the few drinks he'd had to keep him psyched up.

He'd planned only the broad outlines. He could never be bothered with details or plans and in any case, take it as it comes was what always worked best for him, especially in a dangerous situation. His greatest asset was his ability to think fast, on his feet; he was intuitive and able to rely on what his brain dictated at the time. That way you didn't have to cope with unforeseen snags to any pre-arranged plan. All he'd needed was the basic idea and luck, which so far had been with him. But he took that for granted. You made your own luck.

The tricky part was still to come. The night was black as a bag and the rain wasn't helping any. He needed to concentrate on keeping the vehicle steady against the buffeting it was getting. Although the pick-up had good road-holding capacity, the wind-snatch caused it to swerve every time he drove past a gap in the houses. He made a snap decision to avoid the ring road alongside the park and the arboretum. The one thing he didn't need was some uprooted tree to come crashing down on him, especially before he'd jettisoned the cargo he had in the back.

Unless he wanted to deviate miles out of his way, however, he'd no option but to drive through the town centre. For the first time he felt jittery. Hell, it's safe enough, he told himself; power lines were down and whole sections of the town were unlit, the roads were deserted – so far he'd met not a single other person or vehicle. Even the police were keeping a low profile tonight, and who could blame them?

A mega-size piece of brown packaging paper, whirling across the road, forced him to floor the brake pedal. Slapping itself immovably against the windscreen, it immediately reduced his visibility from limited to nil, fouling the wipers so that he couldn't free it that way. He swore, and swung himself out of the driving seat. The wind knocked the breath from his body and nearly had him flat on his back as he fought to get to the front and tear the sodden paper off the glass. He was soaked within seconds and the vehicle rocked dangerously when he swung himself back inside. Rain streamed down the windscreen.

This was bad. So far his mind had been on auto, performing the necessary actions without conscious thought as the need arose, but now he made himself stop and consider. His destination had been the river, the swift-flowing river that would be in spate tonight. Not only in spate, goddamnit, but flooded, especially at the point he'd previously earmarked. He'd never get the vehicle near enough, and carrying a heavy body for any distance in these conditions wasn't an option. Was it fate that had blown the paper across his vision at that particular point? He found he'd stopped at the entrance to Nailers' Yard. A dark and malodorous alley, a place to be avoided, unless you were pretty far gone. But to those who were it was a refuge – to the winos and junkies and destitutes, the no-hopers, the dross of the town, who were glad enough of the free warmth that belched from the ventilation shaft of the Rose's kitchens and the conspicuous waste from its dustbins. The Rose, dignified with the name of casino, was the town's one and only nightclub, and even that was closed early tonight, the light over its side door extinguished.

He slid out of the driving seat again and was practically catapulted into the alley. The main street lights were out here and the darkness was total. The wind shrieked into the narrow space, tin cans rattled, a dustbin lid was lifted several yards and banged down again, sundry other bangs and crashes and the sound of breaking glass came from somewhere in the distance. But in the yard, nothing else moved; no one was there to be disturbed, none of the usual shapeless bundles huddled into cardboard boxes. On this wicked night, even the hardened dossers had seemingly preferred to endure a forced bath in return for a bed at the Sally Army.

He reversed the truck into the alley and let down the tailgate. It took him all his time to keep upright as he dragged the body out the best way he could before finally letting it drop on to the wet granite setts. He was surprised by its relative warmth until he reminded himself how little time had passed since the act.

Breathing heavily, he took a last look around to make sure he'd missed nothing, that no huddled human rubbish had after all been watching from the shadows, but nobody was there to observe him. His idea had been to dump the weighted body in the river, where it would have stayed until nothing remained of it to identify, until any evidence to connect him with it would have disappeared. As it was, this would have to do. He gave the corpse a last look, then left it, stripped of cash, valuables and identification, in the stinking alley, near the side door of the nightclub. Just another mugging victim.

Now that it was all over his cool left him abruptly. His

palms were slippery with sweat and he was suddenly frantic to put as much distance as possible between himself and the alley. He began to drive as though all the devils in hell were after him, but then he forced himself to a more moderate pace. It would be ironic if he had an accident, or was stopped for speeding at this juncture.

In the weeks leading up to this he had repeatedly told himself that if anything went wrong and he was caught – well, that was it, it was the luck of the game – he was willing to pay the penalty. But now it had come to the crunch, he knew there was no way he'd allow himself to be caught. Now that the bastard was dead, why should he sacrifice his own freedom for him?

There was no reason why he should be caught, though. Everything had gone as if pre-ordained . . . A stab in the belly and he'd been gone. Getting him into the back of the truck wasn't nearly as tough as he'd imagined it would be. Making absolutely certain there were no traces left behind had been less easy. He'd been worried about being heard, about the possibility of gurgling water pipes when he drew hot water to clean the blood off the floor and elsewhere, but there'd been no sound from upstairs. He'd gone about the rest of his business undisturbed.

Ten minutes later, he dumped the pick-up back on the building site where it had been left. Builders were notoriously careless with their plant and machinery. The keys had been removed, but that didn't matter. The vehicle didn't exist that he couldn't start without keys if he had to. Despite his struggles against the wind, as he went back down the lane to where he had left his own car hidden, his breathing came more easily. He was safe! He'd won! He'd done what he'd determined to do. He felt a flush of heat, as though he stood under a hot shower, and then the same orgasmic release of tension.

The headlights of the oncoming car transfixed him, the beam pinning him like a moth to a board. For a moment he didn't believe what he was seeing, then realization of what it might mean hit him. His bowels felt loose. There was no way the driver could fail to see him.

He pressed himself back into what little protection the hedge offered as the car bucked past on the bumpy lane, the driver looking fixedly ahead through the segment of windscreen cleared by the wipers. As it passed, the watcher caught a glimpse of a set profile. *What the . . .* ? What the hell was *he* doing out here? Instinct told him to run, but he forced himself to wait, listening for the car coming back, tensing himself to act, but though he stayed there for three, four, maybe five minutes, losing count, his heart thumping like a trip-hammer in his chest, nobody came, and in the end he walked away unchallenged.

He was ninety-nine per cent sure, against all the odds, that he hadn't been seen and recognized by the car driver – but if by some chance he had, he knew exactly what to do about it.

He'd already killed once, so he wouldn't be averse to doing it again.

PART 1

September

1

Long before the big storm, when it was still hot, in mid-September, Christine Wilding stretched out on the edge of the swimming pool in the conservatory, sucking the ice-cube that was all that was left of her lemon drink, gazing moodily into the blue depths as if she might find there the answers she was looking for. All she saw was her own reflection. And while there was nothing much wrong there – springing red-gold hair, slanting turquoise blue eyes and a splendid body – no answers to her problems miraculously appeared.

What problems? What problems did she have, for goodness sake? Married to Jake Wilding for six months and more money to spend than she'd ever had in her life before . . . a spacious, architect-designed home . . . a glamorous lifestyle, with holidays abroad and no restrictions on what she did in her spare time . . . She could think of people who'd welcome problems like that.

Still.

Already the temperature was soaring, although it was barely nine a.m. The sun hadn't yet reached the conservatory so it was just about bearable in there, but the warmth had brought out the overpowering scent of the stephanotis as it climbed to the roof, its waxy, starry white flowers mingling with the old vine planted against the wall. This year, recovering from disturbance by the builders, the vine had borne token fruit again, although the few small bunches were destined never to ripen properly and had begun to wither on the stem. The long, poisonous white trumpets of the datura had all shrivelled and some of them had blown on to the surface of the curved leaf-shaped swimming pool which took up most of the floor space of the conservatory.

Maybe it was just this never-ending heatwave that was getting on her nerves. It seemed ungrateful to complain, but the plain fact was that summer had gone on too long. The endless days of sunshine had begun by being gloriously welcome but by now, into September, had turned to drought and oppressive heat, tediously un-British and very trying to the temper.

Jake alone revelled in the hot weather. He could lie for hours in the sun, soaking it up as if it were the fuel he needed for his amazing energy. He was happy in the summer. Usually, he was.

But he wasn't himself lately. That much was obvious to Christine, if to no one else. For some reason Jake, who normally roared like a lion when things went wrong, expecting ego-smoothing sympathy from everyone else, was keeping quiet. This worried Christine. However much she tried to dismiss it, the idea was beginning to nag at her that he might, for reasons not yet apparent, be having regrets about their marriage.

Her own expectations hadn't been unrealistic and so she hadn't been disappointed. She was thirty-nine and she wasn't a dreamer, having had to fend for herself and Lindsay ever since her divorce from Lindsay's father sixteen years ago. Her immediate acceptance, when Jake had asked her to marry him, had been uncharacteristic but by no means uncertain. They had everything necessary to make a go of it – good sex, an easy companionship. And though she'd never kidded herself that Jake was madly in love with her, he had warmth and generosity enough to make up for that. They'd both known what they wanted. On her part, security for herself and Lindsay; on Jake's, a supportive wife. Marrying again hadn't been on her agenda, and she'd known him such a short time, but she'd had no hesitation in accepting. No, she hadn't been disappointed . . . but had he?

Something had subtly changed. Jake, normally open about most things, suddenly had secrets. That telephone call, for instance, yesterday morning, just after breakfast.

'Who was it? Nigel?' she'd asked as he put the bedroom phone extension down.

'Mm.'

'What did he want, so early?'

'Oh, nothing much.'

He'd buried his head in his wardrobe, making an unnecessary fuss out of selecting which of his extensive – not to say expensive – range of suits to wear. She'd decided then that the call had probably been about Matthew – Jake had his son, Matthew, on his mind in the same way that Christine had Lindsay on hers. But obviously he had his reasons for keeping it to himself, and she didn't intend to press him. You learned to be careful in a second marriage.

She had stood up and slipped into the simple yellow silk sheath she was wearing for the coffee morning, a dazzling and daring shade for one with her colouring. Jake had bought it for her, and Christine was getting used to it. 'My zip, Jake, would you mind? It's a real fiend, this one.'

He came over to her and zipped her up and she smiled at his reflection in the mirror. A big, fairish man with a rugged face and a nose that had once been broken. Brown eyes and a magnetic smile, a slight cleft in his chin. His fingers lingered on the back of her neck. He hesitated. 'I love you, Christine,' he'd said quietly, dropping a kiss lightly on her hair before moving away.

He didn't have to say that, and she wished he hadn't. It was generous of him, a typically impulsive Jake gesture, but it had made her feel marginally worse. She had been close to tears. It wasn't part of the bargain to pretend things you didn't feel.

The coffee morning hadn't been a success. It was in aid of some charity Christine had never heard of, at the house of someone she'd only briefly met before, a whistle stop on the bridge, golf and coffee morning circuit. Everyone there seemed to know everyone else and she'd felt awkward and left out, conspicuous in her yellow frock and bright hair. It was partly her own fault; although normally she enjoyed talking to people and got along with most of them, she really couldn't summon up the effort to respond to the meaningless chit-chat that passed for conversation and had left as soon as she decently could.

At that moment, the mobile telephone warbled by her ear.

'Lindsay, darling! Talk about telepathy! I'd just been thinking of you. How was Italy? I'm dying to hear about it. When? This weekend? Wonderful, I'll put pistachio ice-cream on my shopping list and meet you off the usual train. See you at four-twenty.'

'Oh, Mum, you and your lists!'

Christine was immeasurably glad that Lindsay seemed able to laugh again.

She looked at her watch, decided there was no rush, poured herself another long, cool glass of lemonade and sat up with her arms round her knees, wondering idly about meals for the weekend, looking up the extravagant curving stone staircase that led into the house, telling herself again how lucky she was.

The conservatory into which the swimming pool had been built was the sole remnant of the original early Victorian house upon whose site the present house had been built – by Jake, who was a builder and developer. The first sight of house and garden had left Christine speechless: the split-level white building that was mostly window, set on a slope, the swimming pool in the ornate conservatory below, the tennis court. Recovering herself, she'd rather tactlessly asked what the original house had been like? Hadn't it been worth restoring? There had been an awkward moment. *Jake* was being questioned. Then he'd dismissed the idea with a laugh and one of his grand, expansive gestures, forgetting that building the new house had nearly bankrupted him. What with dry rot and wet rot, unmentionable plumbing and a kitchen like a morgue, it had not, he said. He produced a photograph to prove it where, however, these drawbacks were not apparent. A charming old house, a relatively simple structure with none of the later excesses of the period. But modern was good, and new was very good, with Jake. And the inside of the new house, it had to be admitted, was better than the outside – much better now that she was gradually redecorating and furnishing it, using her considerable flair and

20

attention to the sort of detail Jake couldn't be bothered with. Matthew still called the house Villa del Eldorado. But it was all a matter of taste. Lindsay, for instance, adored it.

The neglected garden with its rusty old laurels and gloomy yews was yet to be tackled and Jake, pleased with what she'd achieved inside the house, had agreed to leave this to her. Undaunted by the prospect, Christine, who'd never owned a garden in her life, was already reading up on the subject, making copious notes, asking advice, ready for when the cooler weather and the time for planting came.

Not too much change, she thought: the unchecked growth of beech and ash saplings, for instance, had grown into a pretty little coppice where all sorts of wild flowers grew. Sometimes at dusk small, chestnut-brown muntjak deer came down to graze at the edge of the wood that bordered the property, and occasionally even jumped the fence into the garden, though they were too shy to let her get near enough even to photograph them. Once or twice at night she had heard their peculiar bark, weird and ghostly and faintly chilling.

She had gradually eased herself into what was for her a very different way of living, though she knew that, ultimately, all this would not be enough. She'd worked all her life and was incapable of dribbling her time away.

It would have been a different story if Nigel had kept his promises. Christine knew that was the major reason for her present restlessness and dissatisfaction. Nigel's image came into her mind: dark, urbane and immaculate. Polished, tanned skin, deep-set eyes, a sophisticated and rather devious man.

Damn Nigel.

In the sapphire-blue swimsuit her body gleamed like a kingfisher's as she stood up in one lithe movement, dived into the pool and swam, fast and with some style, several times across its length. As was usual with Christine, action made her feel temporarily better. It was not being able to do anything about a worrying situation which defeated her.

*   *   *

21

Something was in the wind, the old man was sure. Nigel had on his new dark suit and a pale grey shirt and wore the heavy gold cufflinks and the Roman-mounted lapis-lazuli intaglio ring which an hour earlier had been reposing in the display case; he looked prosperous and urbane – not, however, as self-assured as usual. He was slightly on edge, and he'd given Matthew the day off. Taken together, the signs were that something was going on that he didn't wish either Matthew or George to know about.

'How's your pill supply, Father? Wouldn't it be as well to slip round this afternoon and get Ison to top it up? Can't afford to find yourself without, you know,' he suggested to George, critically assessing the large professional flower arrangement which had just been delivered, one of which was always kept by the door of Cedar House Antiques. Nigel was extremely particular about the impressions such things made. Although the shop was still fitted in the quietly opulent style his grandfather had created – an Edwardian elegance that formed a perfect backdrop for the sparkling gems they sold – he saw to it that it was beautifully kept and decorated. A grey carpet and pale walls, champagne nets and dark blue velvet drapes at the side windows, through which could be seen a glimpse of the big cedar tree on the lawn outside the white, Georgian building; the old display cases also lined with dark blue velvet, a discreet glassed-in office at the back of the shop. Tasteful in a conservative, under-stated style – if too overstocked, in George's opinion. Nigel was inclined to buy what he personally coveted and was then unable to bring himself to sell it.

He answered Nigel's suggestion with a tetchiness in his voice he heard too often lately. 'I'm not so senile yet that I can't look after my own welfare. I've already arranged with Ison to let me have more pills.'

Nigel said nothing more for the time being, point taken, but looking up from his desk a little while later, he remarked, 'Do me a favour, Father, would you, and walk along to Oundle's this afternoon and pick up that new reference book I ordered? They rang this morning to say it'll be there by four.'

Pills! Reference books! A visitor was expected, without doubt. Quite possibly female, and if so, young. Nigel had always been very attractive to women. He had a way of looking at them which conveyed a genuine interest in what they said and did, and a smile, deeply indented at the corners, that they seemed to find irresistible. They passed through his life regularly, in greater numbers than he let on, but conforming to a certain type. He liked to maintain the fiction that these affairs were not generally known about, certainly not to his father. George, though uneasy about them, didn't disabuse him. In his own way, he could be as cagey as Nigel.

He's my father all over, George thought, pottering about, covertly watching his son: Henri Fontenoy as he was when he took over the business from his father, Edouard, the founder of what had then been Fontenoy Gems. Shrewd and go-ahead and, in Nigel's case, confident enough to be forever urging his father to expand, even in these difficult times. Not content with branching out into selling silver and small antiques, as well as fine old jewellery. But George (he'd dropped the 's' at the end of his given name years ago; the family was British now, and proud of it) was stubborn, and clung to the old ways. That one disastrous foray into modern jewellery, many years ago, wasn't something he was anxious to repeat.

Nigel remained uncharacteristically fidgety for the rest of the morning, making from time to time further suggestions as to how George might occupy himself during the afternoon, but George had no desire to go out. He wanted to stay where he was, in the shop, his place for over fifty years, if only to be there should any customer need his specialist advice on what piece of jewellery to buy. And, incidentally, to find out what Nigel was up to; although, in effect, George accepted that he no longer had the automatic right to expect to be told every little thing. His world had lately changed to a place where he was not the one who gave the orders, a fact he'd been forced to accept since his stroke. It was Nigel who was now in charge.

'I might wander up and see Christine,' he said at last, putting Nigel out of his misery, adding that he'd better make

23

the most of this hot weather. Couldn't go on much longer, it must break soon, which would mean he'd be confined indoors. He was committed, since his stroke, to taking regular exercise, and though he affected to despise doctors, Ison was a sound man whose advice George usually took, if sometimes with bad grace.

'Good idea,' Nigel replied, over-hearty with relief, 'but I should get her to drive you back. The walk there's quite far enough.'

George knew himself quite capable of walking both ways, and that it would be good for him to do so. The heat didn't affect him – at his age, the problem was keeping warm enough. He didn't say so, or remind Nigel that Christine, when he'd spoken to her on the telephone not an hour since, had said that Lindsay was coming home for the weekend. And since she always met Lindsay off the four-twenty, she wouldn't be at home. It would do no harm, however, to lull Nigel into thinking he would be out of the shop for the time it took to walk along to Ham Lane and back, plus half an hour or so for a cup of tea when he got there. Evidently that would serve to keep George away long enough, or would have done if George had had any intention of making the abortive visit, which he had not.

2

Earlier that same morning, walking down to the site office after parking the car, Jake's immediate attention had been caught by the sight of Matthew, deep in conversation with Joss Graham over the engine of one of his bright yellow lorries, WILDING painted in two-foot letters down the sides. His first pleased surprise at seeing Matthew there was immediately quenched when he saw the animation drain from the boy's face as he looked up and saw his father.

Jake's reaction to how much this hurt put him wrong-footed from the start. 'If you *must* smoke, don't do it here, and certainly not over that petrol tank,' he said shortly. 'You should both know better.' They put out their cigarettes, Joss immediately, his attractive, lazy smile apologetic – he knew smoking was forbidden, for obvious reasons, and wasn't normally either insubordinate or foolish. Matthew, however, only put his out after taking another defiant pull. 'I'd like a word, Matthew, in the office. If you can spare a minute.'

Jake, raising his voice above a churning cement mixer and the sound of another lorry depositing a load of hard-core, realized too late how the words would sound to Matthew. Tact was not his middle name, he reflected wryly, as he walked to the portakabin that served as site office, red dust rising in little puffs round his feet. He heard the boy's reluctant footsteps behind him and could visualize the resentment already building up. Hell's teeth! He tried to remind himself to tread as though on eggshells whenever he spoke to Matthew and yet he heard himself saying all the wrong things, to which Matthew predictably responded, either with one of his smart-alec retorts or faintly veiled insolence. He never acted that way with anyone else. It was a phase he was going through, everyone said. He'd been such an appealing little boy; remember what pals he and Jake had always been?

The implication being, Jake felt, that it had all been his fault. Yet however hard he tried, Jake couldn't seem to get through any more. Adolescent behaviour he could just about cope with, but this bloody-mindedness was something else. Matthew was, after all, nearly nineteen.

He'd long since dismissed the notion that Matthew resented his marriage to Christine, or was jealous of his affection for Lindsay, they all got on too well. But Jake's divorce had happened when Matthew was a mere baby and he'd never discussed the details with Matthew: why Naomi had left him for another man, leaving him to fulfil the role of both parents. In fact, it hadn't been until he was already entering his teens that Matthew had showed any sort of curiosity about his mother. Yet to discuss Naomi's faults and imperfections with a vulnerable thirteen-year-old boy hadn't seemed like a good idea, then or now; Jake had skirted the subject, finding it impossible to explain the disaster that had been Naomi to him. Impossible to explain Naomi to anyone! Christine had suggested that maybe Matthew blamed Jake for what had gone wrong. It would have been a disturbing thought, if true. Jake didn't believe it, however. That wasn't the main reason for Matthew's present intransigence.

Reaching the temporary office, he turned to wait for his son before pushing open the office door.

'Morning, Thelma.'

'Morning, Mr Wilding. Nice to see you, Matthew.'

Thelma must have seen Jake arrive on site. Another gooey layer had been added to her lipstick, her library book pushed into a drawer and coffee, the rich dark brew she knew he liked, was already made. He felt, as usual, exasperated with her. He'd told her he didn't mind what she did on the days when she worked here and not at his main office in town. Whether she knitted, read her library romances, filed her nails or twiddled her thumbs, as long as the work was done – and God knows, there was little enough of that to keep

26

her fully occupied at the moment. Thelma, however, middle-aged, widowed and motherly, had old-fashioned ideas about keeping up appearances. She reached for another mug as Matthew came in with his father and carried the coffee on a tray into the adjoining office. A plate of her home-made Shrewsbury biscuits came with it. There was a single yellow rose in a crystal bud vase set incongruously on the rough table that served as a desk.

Matthew reached for a biscuit and took a large bite. 'Mmm. Brilliant!' In fact, the biscuits were nothing special. Good and wholesome, but nothing particularly out of the way. But being charming (to everyone except his father) was a natural part of Matthew's likeable personality, one that endeared him to everyone – especially females, judging by his string of girlfriends. Even Thelma, normally immune to flattery, was smiling plummily back.

When she had poured the coffee and left them to it, Jake remarked, 'To what do we owe this honour, Matthew? Shouldn't you be at the shop?' He tried to make his tone light but for the life of him he couldn't keep out the derogatory inflexion. Matthew, however, merely shrugged. He was wearing the dark suit and discreet tie he wore for work. He looked extremely personable but curiously out of keeping. A track suit, jeans, casual clothes of any kind was more his style, the style that complemented his outdoor tan, crisp, short dark hair and the compact, athletic figure.

'Cousin Nigel,' he said, 'has decided to give me the day off, in lieu. The policy's to open all hours from now on, even Thursday.'

Jake never could work out what Matthew's real feelings were towards Nigel – not, in fact, *his* cousin, but Jake's – nor what his attitude towards his job with him was. For one thing, he was so damned independent it was difficult to imagine him being beholden to anyone. Another thing was the job itself. Impossible, even a few months ago, to imagine Matt working in the rarefied atmosphere of Fontenoy's. From childhood, it had been difficult to keep him off any site of his father's. He was familiar with everything that was going on, with future plans, he knew everyone, had a working relationship with plant, machinery, the whole works. There had never been any question of him doing anything else but join Jake in the business when he left school.

Jake, who was the first to admit he hadn't the faintest idea how to go about handling this new Matthew, pushed the problem to one side. And belatedly, what Matt had just said about Thursday closing suddenly registered with him.

Thinking about it, he decided that if Nigel was prepared to discard the time-honoured custom of half-day closing mid-week, his claim that he was really feeling the pinch might not be the simple ploy to get the loan repaid that Jake had thought. That didn't mean Nigel had forgotten the bloody loan, however, not he! Or was prepared to extend its repayment. Not that it was a matter of life and death to either of them, but in the circumstances, its recall would be embarrassing. Jake rubbed a hand down his chin and looked speculatively at Matthew. He decided to speak, even at risk of the rebuff he knew would come.

'If he decides to cut down on staff – well, there's always room for you in the business, you know that.' And always would be, even if it meant getting rid of someone else.

'If there *is* –' Matthew began.

'If there *is* a business much longer', was what he'd been going to say, Jake knew. It would have been a perfectly justifiable remark. The building and construction business was, to put it mildly, in the doldrums. He didn't know why Matthew had bitten off the comment – it was too much to believe that he was having qualms of conscience, or even beginning to realize that all this constant sniping was hardly the best way to get round his father.

Matthew had, in fact, hastily broken off the careless words because he knew it was all too easy, these days, to trigger off one of Jake's right royal rages. Admittedly, they never lasted long, but it was smart to avoid them, or to keep your head below the parapet while they did last.

This present site was Phase One of a development of thirty luxuriously fitted, executive-style homes. One or two were actually occupied, a few more spoken for, but despite massive reductions on the original price, most remained unsold. Yet the real fly in the ointment, as far as Jake was concerned, was the other, adjoining site. The ten acres – and on it the derelict house, unoccupied for dozens of years – which Jake had bought with the intention of demolishing, and which had then, by some fancy footwork on the part of local conservationists, had a preservation order slapped on it. So there the old house still stood, where the new Save All hypermarket, which would have been Jake's saviour, should by now have been rising. Save All were becoming restive, there was every prospect they'd pull out of the deal. Jake, the great Jake, had come unstuck. Instead of being one step ahead, as he always prided himself on being, he'd been two steps behind.

But no way was Matthew going to start feeling sorry for Jake! He'd plenty of other irons in the fire. He drained his coffee and said suddenly, standing up, 'Well, as far as Nigel goes, I'm not staff, I'm one of the family. And anyway, it's what I want to do, right?'

'Is it? Is it really?'

They stared at one another, Matthew uptight and aggressive at what he took to be his father's sarcasm, Jake trying so hard not to be that the cords stood out on his neck.

'I have to go. What was it you wanted?' Matthew asked abruptly, carefully avoiding the use of Jake's name. It was as if 'Dad' had become a dirty word lately.

'It can wait. Oh, all right, then,' Jake added as Matt raised his brows. 'I only wondered if it's such a good idea coming on site to see young Graham – maybe it would be better to arrange to see him outside working hours.'

Jake thought he'd couched this as a suggestion rather than an order, but Matthew stiffened. 'I only called in for a minute because he's co-driving for me this weekend and I wanted to fix things up.'

And here they were again. Back to the real crunch point. Rally driving, which was Matthew's current obsession. If he'd had the money he'd have defied Jake and gone for it, not only as the hobby which it presently was, but as a full-time career, which was what he was naive enough to think it could be. It was the root cause of all the trouble between them. Jake had the upper hand at the moment because he held the purse strings, but he knew that was no real answer. 'Fair enough,' he said, for the moment defeated. He was enough at loggerheads with Matt without adding to it over this. He could hardly complain about him coming to the site, when it was the one thing he tried to encourage. Nor could he grumble about his association with Joss Graham, seeing that he approved of so little else about Matthew these days. He liked Joss, with the reservation that he considered he was wasting his training as a microbiologist, working on a building site. But that was his own affair. He was at least willing to work at whatever he could find, and not content to live on the dole, like so many with his educational achievements these days, unable to find a suitable position when they'd qualified. He had an open, friendly manner, he was a hard worker and, as far as Jake could see, no bad influence on Matthew − though Jake had made it plain enough that he didn't consider it wise for them to get too friendly. If Matthew eventually did come into the firm, it would only make matters difficult. 'Fair enough,' he repeated, 'only don't make it too much of a habit.'

Matthew looked sullen, sketched a hasty farewell and Jake watched him roar off in his hotted-up Golf GTI, in a cloud of red dust. An intensely physical person, too interested in cars and sport and outdoor activities of any kind to have made much impression at school, totally uninterested in anything remotely artistic, only a perfect idiot would believe Matthew had any special, burning desire to spend the rest of his life selling antique jewellery.

With another sigh, Jake turned from the window and took his tie off, loosened his collar. It was like an oven in the office. The air was heavy and thundery. Surely this long, hot summer must come to an end sometime.

3

It was just after four and Christine, in a carefully chosen white linen trouser suit with a lot of gold costume jewellery, sat at the wheel of her open-topped Lancia outside the station, waiting for Lindsay.

She was last out of the station, after all the others had gone, shoppers clutching classy green Harrods' bags arriving at the same time as commuters since it was Friday, the day they all left London early to extend the weekend. Lindsay, a music student, had her lute case over one shoulder, her bag on the other. She was carrying a heavy holdall but she appeared as unruffled and cool as ever. She stood hesitating at the entrance, as if unwilling to leave its shelter.

Small and composed, uncreased after a hot and crowded train journey, her straight brown hair drawn back from her face, she was as unlike Christine as it was possible to be. Always neat and tidy, like a little girl dressed for a party, today she was wearing a cream silk shirt and a neat, coffee-coloured linen skirt, her only jewellery a pair of small pearl earrings. She frequently made Christine feel too highly-coloured and three sizes too big. Was it fancy that she looked paler than ever, or was it the heat, always so much more trying in the later summer than it was earlier, which gave her that look of fragile translucency? Oh God, Christine thought, with intuitive perception, she's still not better. They hadn't seen the last of the glandular fever that had plagued Lindsay on and off for the last five or six months, depressing and debilitating her. Her holiday in Italy didn't appear to have done her much good.

'Lovely, lovely to see you, darling!'

'Hello, Mother.' Lindsay held up her face to be kissed and they hugged, smiling. Their only point of resemblance, the wide, dazzling smile, was always a surprising and delightful thing to see on Lindsay's small, habitually grave face, but especially now. Until recently, she and Christine had always been close and had had a loving relationship, despite their differences in temperament; they had, after all, been alone together for sixteen years. But Lindsay, for some inexplicable reason, had closed in on herself during her illness, leaving Christine feeling shut out and unhappy.

She'd always tried to be a conscientious mother, even when she'd had to work to support herself and Lindsay; apart from such considerations as natural affection, Christine couldn't bear not to be efficient at everything, including personal relationships. For the umpteenth time, she wondered where she'd gone wrong with Lindsay as she tied a scarf over her brilliant hair and from the glove compartment handed her daughter one, which Lindsay left on her lap.

The big open car slid along smoothly and very fast, guided by Christine's well-shaped, capable hands on the wheel, moving through imperceptible gear changes and well-anticipated corners, so that Lindsay wasn't thrown around as, for instance, when Matthew drove. After she'd answered the usual detailed questionnaire from Christine: questions ranging from how was Italy, was she eating properly – and receiving truthful answers, for Lindsay never lied directly, only by omission – Lindsay asked politely, to change the subject, 'How's Jake?'

'Busy, what else? Cooking up schemes. You know Jake.' Christine negotiated a tricky intersection where the main road crossed the country lane they were travelling along. 'He has something on his mind.'

'What sort of thing?'

'Wish I knew! Business, I expect, it's not doing as well as he'd like.'

'The recession –'

'What are we all going to blame our troubles on when the recession's over?' Christine laughed lightly, grew silent for a while, then resumed her chatter, bringing Lindsay up to date with the latest news, while the hedges rushed dizzily past in the wind generated by the car's passing.

Lindsay, feeling washed out and colourless beside her mother, who always looked so stunning, wished she wouldn't talk so much, wouldn't drive so fast. Not that Christine took risks. It was just that she would have liked the opportunity to be able to drink in the quiet countryside, today looking amazingly green after thirsty, dusty brown London, although the hot summer had brought the first touches of autumn early here, too. More than that, she needed quiet, to be alone in her head for a while before facing them all again.

'Are you sure you're all right, darling?' Christine asked suddenly and Lindsay, jerked out of her introspection, replied too quickly that of course she was, and there was a tight silence of the sort Christine had become only too used to before the last time Lindsay had gone away.

She sometimes thought that having a conversation with her daughter was like unravelling an old jersey for reknitting. For row after row the stitches would streel smoothly away and then would come a snarl, the wool would break off and have to be tied together again. Christine's family had been poor and she had too many memories of having to wear reknit jerseys, the wrong side full of knots which invariably worked through to the front, to be comfortable with the analogy.

Lindsay sat on her bed, feeling suspended, floating. Her luggage was still unpacked, dumped on the floor, reminding her of another time she'd been here, alone in her room with her suitcase packed.

A horrible time. It had nearly been too much for her, the misery had threatened to take her over, so that she had no will of her own. She had thought, hopelessly: my life's out of control. Not to be in control of yourself and your actions was just about the worst scenario she could imagine. Perhaps she ought never to have gone away, alone. She'd always been like a chameleon, taking on the colour of her surroundings. In London, in her dreary and depressing little flat, dark and unacceptable ideas took possession of her. It was only through her music, by throwing herself into her studies, that she had kept sane, but here in this lovely, light-filled house she felt boundless peace, a renewal of energy and a possibility that the future might actually have something in store for her. Italy had helped her to get herself together again, the last dark months were over . . . One hurdle was already over, the most difficult: Christine, who always seemed to see right through her, right to the bone. Now there was only Matthew, who was all right, no need to worry about him. And Jake, who was the nearest she'd yet found to a father.

She picked up her lute and strummed a desultory chord or two, breathing deeply until she was calm enough to go downstairs.

But still she hesitated. And presently, she found herself reluctantly reaching out for the morocco box on her dressing table where she kept her small collection of 'real' jewellery, the Victorian pieces she loved, all of them presents: the turquoise necklace from her mother, the delicate gold and seed pearl cluster ring Nigel had given her for her eighteenth birthday, the hair brooch and the pretty pair of tiny Victorian coral drop earrings from Jake. She scarcely ever had occasion to wear them, but they were there if ever she did. They were the only kinds of jewellery she really liked.

Finally, she took a small flat package from her shoulder bag. After staring at it uneasily for several minutes, she pushed it into the box underneath the jewellery.

From outside came the sound of a motorbike drawing up on the gravel by the front door. She jumped up to look out of the window. Cassie!

In two minutes she was downstairs.

Christine, taking a bowl of salad from the kitchen to the dining room, heard the cries of welcome and stopped to watch the two girls through the open dining room door. For a moment she felt a stab of jealousy. How long was it since Lindsay had been so forthcoming with her? What was it about this strong, stocky girl with her smouldering dark eyes, her mass of black hair and, let it be said, her sometimes undesirable manners, that so attracted Lindsay? She didn't care who she offended and seemed oblivious of the fact that Jake neither liked her nor made her welcome. She would certainly invite herself to supper, and Christine wasn't best pleased about that; apart from buying the pistachio ice-cream Lindsay doted on, she'd gone to some trouble to prepare a special meal. There was just enough, which would mean eking out. Cassie ate a lot, as Christine knew to her cost, for she'd continued to come here in Lindsay's absence, having somehow formed an odd sort of friendship with Matthew as well. Friendship was all it was, Christine didn't believe there was anything more than that between them. Cassie Andreas was secretive; despite the fact that she'd been coming to the house on and off for several months, Christine knew virtually nothing about her, except that she was half Greek and that she and her mother had only recently come to live in England, and that Cassie now worked part time on the petrol pumps at the Esso station down the road – and most of this had been dragged out of either Matthew or Lindsay. It wouldn't have made her feel any better to learn that neither of them knew much more about Cassie than she did – the difference being that it didn't matter to them.

Ostensibly watching *Friday Night with Callaghan* with Jake, after the two girls and Matthew had wedged themselves into Matt's car and roared away like 1920s bright young things, Christine found herself thinking again about the situation and growing tight-lipped. The time for finesse had gone. This was their house, hers and Jake's, Matthew and Lindsay were their children. As parents, she and Jake had a right to know who it was they brought home.

'Good, isn't he?' Jake broke into her thoughts, lounging back and watching Tom Callaghan on the box, a suave figure with wavy, prematurely white hair and twinkling grey eyes. The show was very popular at the moment, the ratings were high. Jake liked to watch it because Callaghan was his old school chum, one of a once inseparable trio: Jake, Tom and Jake's cousin, Nigel Fontenoy. That was possibly why Jake wasn't as critical of the programme as Christine, but didn't explain why millions of others liked the show, too. Christine, however, wondered how long it would last. Callaghan probed serious issues, but with a smiling urbanity and an impression of such thorough investigation, that his viewers were left with the comfortable feeling of being absolved from the disagreeable necessity of having to do anything personally about it.

Tonight, he had been interviewing victims of street crime – mugging, assault, rape, one survivor of a bomb attack. The rape victim was being asked whether she didn't honestly think it possible that some women did in fact provoke such attacks by the way they dressed. The woman answered shortly that no, she didn't, women had the right to dress as they wished, less than delighted with the hoary old question but looking Callaghan straight in the eye. The camera zoomed in on her tight red top, short leather skirt and long, long legs. 'I'm sure we all agree with you,' said Tom Callaghan sincerely, and launched smoothly into his wind-up speech and all-purpose smile.

The credits began to roll and Christine went into the kitchen to make some tea. She'd long ago decided she didn't like Tom Callaghan.

Arriving home that night after the show, Callaghan felt an immense weariness. He switched on the lamps and set the air-conditioning as high as it would go, threw his jacket across a chair back and took off his tie and his shoes. Then he poured two inches of Glenfiddich and made himself a ham sandwich. He could never eat before or immediately after the show, his stomach was too screwed up, but by now he was hungry. He could have eaten a good solid meal but his wife had recently walked out on him, and in any case, had never bothered to cook. He was nothing of a cook, himself.

He sat on the sofa to eat his sandwich, allowing his gaze to rest for a while on the photograph on his desk, a thing he always did every time he came back home, as if by doing so he might will the subject of it to materialize. It was the only photograph in the room.

The big picture window gave on to the river; the view was one of the best things about the flat, which was bare, almost monastic, as he preferred it, now that Joanna had taken with her all the fancy bits and pieces. What furnishings remained were plain but good, chosen by him. He had grown up with the second rate, but he knew a good thing when he saw it. He was careful over what he bought, canny with money. He had made – and was still making – plenty, but, as he well knew and heeded, there were fashions in celebrities, as in anything else. Nothing lasted.

He sipped his whisky and slowly he began to relax. The show took more out of him every time. You had to be alert and on your toes the whole time, to think fast, though he was naturally a quick and agile thinker, as journalists have to be. In his game, you couldn't afford to miss a trick, you could allow yourself to forget nothing. That never bothered him, however. His memory was phenomenal. And there were some things no one ever forgot, or forgave. A ghost from the past laid a gentle hand on his shoulder, but it wasn't his runaway wife's. He felt a warning of the recurrent pain in his head, the one that had signalled trouble ever since he was a child, that he'd always been wise not to ignore. He shivered in the air-conditioning and thought it was a night to go to bed with a pill.

Sleep didn't come easily, however. Tonight, as so often, he was haunted by memories from the past.

His father, Rory Callaghan, had been an Irish Protestant dockworker of the Ian Paisley persuasion, who believed in hell fire and damnation, who had never forgiven himself his own lapse in marrying a foreigner, nor her either. Marietta had been a bright, volatile, clever woman, and though Italian, not religious, who could make his bigoted opinions look ridiculous, and frequently did as it became more and more apparent that their marriage was a disaster. Religion had not been the only source of their strife, however. There had been plenty more.

Yet – for the sake of the child, Tom, it was said – they'd stuck together until Rory had died, mercifully for Marietta though not for Rory, of a stomach cancer. Marietta had come to England, found herself a series of jobs teaching Italian, the last of which had brought her to Lavenstock. And there

Tom had stayed, too, working first on various local newspapers, going on to radio and graduating to television.

His parents' marriage had been an explosive combination, and Tom's childhood hadn't been happy. The two strands of his inheritance still warred too much in him, irking him like the failure of his marriage, though he allowed none of it to inhibit him professionally. His public persona, and his private one, he had always kept as strictly apart as possible, for the very good reason that his private life contained a grief so huge it encompassed him entirely, one that could never be shared by anyone.

He fell asleep, as he did most nights, his mind feeding on the great wrong that had been done, to dream, as always, of revenge.

Jake was singing as he washed the breakfast dishes, his shirt sleeves rolled up. It was not an image associated with his tough, public one.

The kitchen windows were steamy, bubbles flew as he squirted detergent into the hot water with abandon. He enjoyed washing up, he said it was therapeutic. He sang in the kitchen like other people sang in the bath, ritually, his not very tuneful baritone belting out songs from his youth, or from the latest show.

'*Yesterday. All my troubles seemed so far away –*' he sang under his breath, off key, plunging muscular, hairy forearms into the sinkful of hot, soapy water.

'You've put too much Fairy Liquid in,' Christine said, annoyed, picking up a teatowel and wiping the suds off a plate. 'And what's wrong with the dishwasher?'

'Doesn't do the saucepans properly.'

'You could wash up twenty times with that amount.'

'If that's all you're bothered about, I'll buy you another bottle, for God's sake. *And I believe in yes-ter-day.*'

'Jake –!'

Last night they'd been lovers and this morning here they were, washing up and bickering like any old married couple, she thought, dispirited, as she turned to put a pile of plates away.

'Hey, what's the matter?'

She felt his arms round her waist from the back and leaned into him. 'Oh, I'm sorry, I'm sorry. But Jake –'

'Hm?' He nuzzled his chin into her shoulder.

She turned herself round in his arms. 'Jake, we have to talk. Please don't try to put me off again.'

'About?'

'About Cassie. I think we ought to know more about her.' She had a sense of urgency about this that she didn't quite understand. 'I'd like to meet her mother.'

Jake was silent for a while. 'I need notice of that question,' he said eventually, 'though personally I don't see any point in it. If it's Matt you're worried about, forget it. He's more interested at the moment in long-legged blondes with nothing much between their ears than in Cassie Andreas.'

'I'm not worried in that way! Not when their sole topic of conversation's compression ratios and overhead camshafts and differentials –'

Jake gave a snort of laughter.

'But I'd still like to meet that mother of hers.'

'Leave it. Let things take their course.' Jake was terse. There was a warning there, if she had heeded it. 'Anyway, I'll bet you wouldn't – like to meet her, that is. It seems to me that one Andreas is more than enough.'

4

It was shady in the plot at the back of the brick house above the railway embankment, and quiet enough between trains, though they ran for most of the twenty-four hours, the big InterCity ones whooshing by every half hour, gone in an instant. Each time any one of them passed, the unsteady little house, erected by the railway with other, now derelict buildings at the turn of the century for some obscure and long-forgotten purpose, seemed to have moved one step nearer total extinction.

Outside at the back, there were three old apple trees which, in a garden of this size, made the kitchen as dark as Hades, but they were already heavy with the early-ripened fruit of this hot summer. A great many apples had dropped off and lay rotting on the ground, giving off a boozy, cidery smell. The untended, uncut grass where Naomi walked was shiveringly sensuous and cool under her bare feet. They were long and elegant feet, brown but not very clean.

She was wearing an ankle length granny print cotton skirt with a deep frill round the hem that she'd had for maybe twenty years, and an embroidered cotton blouse brought home from a far-off holiday in the Greek islands with that painter whose name she'd forgotten. She'd had a lot of style when she was younger and still had when she took the trouble, though she was beginning to do that less and less. Her hair was grey and untidy, tucked carelessly behind her ears. She had a long, aquiline face and she would never see forty again. It wasn't until you noticed her very beautiful grey eyes and the lovely bone structure that you realized why she had once been considered beautiful.

Sitting on the ground in the shade of one of the trees, leaning against its rough bark, she ate her lunch, consisting of a handful of fresh dates, a carob bar and a glass of wine, while reluctantly bringing her mind to the problem of what she must do. She was in an impossible situation and knowing that she'd brought it on herself made it no better. She didn't waste time in self-recrimination . . . she was too used to bringing trouble to her own door by now to blame herself when it happened.

All the same, it wouldn't have happened if she hadn't come back to England, or at least to this part of it. Why had she, when she could have gone anywhere? In retrospect, it was easy to see that it was bound to cause complications. But she'd always been fond of the place, and when her mother had died and left her the house at a time when she was homeless and nearly penniless it had seemed crass stupidity to refuse to return and live in it. After all, they were all civilized people. She couldn't see that it would matter to Jake now. And she'd wanted to see Matthew. She had a right to see him. He was, let's face it, she thought, her own flesh and blood, her son – conveniently forgetting that she'd never sent him so much as a birthday card in eighteen years.

She should have approached Jake before this. But she hadn't, and now . . . What was she going to do about Matthew and Cassie? Jesus, Mary and Joseph! Who could have imagined *that* happening?

How serious was it, with Cassie and Matthew? How did you find out if your daughter was sleeping with her boy-friend? Well, just ask! That was easy, it was what she'd always done before, anyway, though she'd been too stunned when Cassie had produced Matthew last night to probe too deeply. Suddenly, out of the blue, 'This is Matthew, Matthew Wilding.' Besides, they'd had that owl-eyed girl, Lindsay, with them.

But supposing she asked and got the answer yes; how could she then tell Cassie that her boyfriend was also her half-brother?

She was going to have to do something – instantly – to prevent catastrophe – if it wasn't already too late. Panic almost overcame the sense of enormous ennui engendered by the thought of having to act. She was very good at putting things off, even better at doing nothing at all. The lotus-eating life she'd led since leaving Jake had suited her temperament down to the ground, a temperament she certainly hadn't passed on. She couldn't imagine how she'd come to have three children so energetic and decisive.

Despite his dark hair, Matthew was so like Jake, with the immediately recognizable family nose, that she had known and recognized him as her son instantly, almost before Cassie had introduced him last night, and she'd been shocked at the uprush of emotion. She was very sorry indeed, at that moment, that she'd ever left him and vowed she must do something to compensate.

The thought of facing Jake after all this time didn't alarm her – Naomi was alarmed by very little – but for a moment, as she thought of the consequences which might possibly follow, her resolution did falter. But it would surely be all right if she did what she had to immediately, without thinking too long about it. She was a creature of impulse. That was how the decision to leave Jake had come about: she'd suddenly become fed up with being a wife, and for Naomi there was nothing so dead as something which no longer caught her interest.

She'd always hated being tied down and had lived in a joyously free and what some might have called unprincipled way until she'd met Jake again and decided to marry him. Handsome Jake, who had only needed to smile and she was done for. It had been possible to make herself believe she could become the nice, obedient, responsible wife he wanted. And it *had* worked for a while, until she began to feel stifled with too many possessions, too much money. Jake had adored her, and the baby, when he came, was absolutely delicious. But then he'd begun teething and he'd had whooping cough and was fretful and tetchy after it, and wasn't quite so delicious any longer. The novelty of her new lifestyle had quickly begun to wear off, coincidentally with two other things happening. First, Ty Andreas had come into her life, via the Greek restaurant where he worked as a waiter. Then her mother's new husband had written to order Naomi from then on to take responsibility for her elder child, the one she'd never told Jake about. He said it was high time her mother had the opportunity to enjoy a life of her own, she shouldn't be saddled with someone else's six-year-old, it wasn't right at her age. It had been time to pick up the child and move on.

Naomi hadn't initially intended her decampment to be permanent. One day she would come back to Jake and Matthew, of course she would; but somehow the years, mostly in Greece but also on the island of Corfu, Italy, America, Spain, had stretched out. And even after Ty had been killed in a taverna brawl and she'd left the others (or they'd left her) she hadn't been able to summon up the energy to return. By then, she and Jake were divorced, anyway.

Since then, there had always been problems with money, but that was something which had never been important to her and she'd grown used to managing on hardly anything. She never seriously considered taking up her work again where she'd left off, although she'd had talent – oh yes, outstanding talent, it had been said more than once. You needed more than that to succeed, however – hard work and stickability, for instance – concepts which bored Naomi. In the end, the money had run out completely and even her Micawberish view of life began to waver. Nothing – or, as was more usual in Naomi's case – nobody, had turned up to save her this time. Until her mother had left her the house.

'It's good. It's good to be here and not always going somewhere else,' said Cassie, child of too many disruptive moves, after they had settled in. 'We should stay here.'

'Well, we'll see. It all depends.'

It was a very small house, though it had three bedrooms if you counted the attic. But the unexpected legacy had given them shelter for the last months, if no income, and the house, occupied for years by various tenants, was in a terrible condition. Unspeakable things must be happening under the roof slates, because the ceilings were sagging; some of the floors were rotten, paint was peeling everywhere and the front fence was falling down. Naomi's housekeeping was sluttish, and she could easily shut her eyes to the state of the house, but she was still practically on her beam ends, so much so that she'd put the house on the market. She hadn't even had a nibble. The sign still stood, planted drunkenly in the front plot, bindweed climbing up its post and threatening to obliterate its message.

Oh, she'd been mad, mad to come back! And not least because Nigel might well hear of her return. She was putty in the hands of any persuasive man, and Nigel was nothing if not persuasive. And, she had no need to remind herself, very nasty when roused.

But what could he do? Automatically, she touched the wood of the tree trunk. All her life she'd been irredeemably superstitious, believing implicitly in luck, good or bad. It was astonishing that she still had the one thing he had coveted, intact, that it had survived all that had happened to her, that she hadn't lost or misplaced it somewhere along the way. Most of everything else she'd ever possessed was scattered somewhere around the globe, marking her progress like an animal's spoor.

And anyway, he probably had no need of it now, after all these years. But she knew Nigel and his persistence and was tempted briefly, just for a second. Why not give in and be done with it? It was of no conceivable use to her; she would, in fact, feel much more comfortable without it.

Then her resolution hardened again, she felt vindictive. Nigel thought that money could buy everything. Giving in to him would be the last – the very last – thing she would do.

A little, cold wind had sprung up, and she shivered. A fifteen-coach express, *en route* from Birmingham, the second city, to London, the first, pounded past. The house shook, then creaked and groaned itself quiet. The fence leaned over a little more. It would soon be winter again. Naomi wondered how much longer they could survive here.

5

Jake recognized the handwriting on the envelope as soon as he saw it. It gave him a nasty, unpleasant jolt, though at the back of his mind he'd been expecting something like this. He thrust it into his pocket to read in private, but when he arrived at his main offices in the town, a golden-windowed tower block, the latest prestigious development next to the new shopping precinct, he was still reluctant to read it. He let it stay there all day in his pocket, burning a hole, until he was alone and unlikely to be disturbed, until everyone but the cleaners had gone home, the word processors and the fax machines were silent and the only sound was the distant drone of vacuum cleaners.

Naomi's beautiful cursive handwriting stared at him, dark and bold, and so large that the little she had to say took several pages. What the message amounted to was that she was living less than seven miles from him, with her son and her daughter, Cassie. He stared at the letter. Well, yes. He had known who Cassie Andreas must be the moment he heard her name – Andreas had been the name of that Greek waiter Naomi had run off with. But he'd done nothing about it, convinced that the problem would go away of its own accord, that Naomi would disappear as suddenly as she'd arrived, just as she'd always done. How naive could you get?

The letter went on to say that Naomi had recently met Matthew but hadn't (thank God) yet told him who she was. He would have to know, however, because – Jake must have noticed this – he and Cassie were obviously becoming attached to each other, and not as brother and sister, either. Naomi was prepared to tell them the facts, if Jake was not.

They ought to know – although she was in any case leaving Lavenstock just as soon as she could sell her house, and would take Cassie with her. Of course, she couldn't speak for her son, Joss, but he'd surely go with them, too. He'd always been a rolling stone and was long overdue for a move.

Joss. Joss Graham.

Jake threw the letter on to the desk as if it had suddenly become contagious, pushed his chair back, poured himself a glass of Glen Morangie from the private supply he kept for entertaining, and went to stare out of the windows, which were not golden at all inside, but dull. The anti-glare glass meant an absence of sunlight, which had come to depress Jake, though he'd been responsible for it, for the whole development, in fact. He was already contemplating other premises.

There was a PS to the letter. Nigel was *not* to know that Naomi was in Lavenstock.

What the hell was she up to? A spot of not-so-subtle black-mail? *As soon as I can sell my house.* He immediately rejected the idea. Naomi, whatever her other faults, was the least mercenary person he'd ever known. Jake drained his glass and chewed his lip, and went back to reread the letter, not the bit about Cassie and Matthew, which didn't worry him in the least. Matthew couldn't possibly be attracted to that wretched girl, he thought dismissively, projecting his own feelings about her on to his son without too much consideration of the matter. But what about Joss?

Graham as a surname wasn't unusual, and Jake had never remotely connected him with Naomi, nor with Cassie; why should he? Presumably Matthew (and Lindsay, for that matter) knew the two were brother and sister, but there was no reason why they should have connected them with him as anything other than Joss's employer. And Cassie had been the only one to visit the house, never Joss: Jake had made his views on how things stood in that direction plain enough, after all.

He began to calculate Joss's age. Born, he noted sardoni-cally, before he, Jake, had married Naomi. Not, however, before he had first met her. Naomi-like, she'd disappeared for several years after their first meeting, and then returned to Lavenstock. It was only then that they had rediscovered each other and married. But even so, what he suspected, that she was belatedly trying to foist parental responsibility for Joss on to him, was improbable, but certainly not, he feared, impossible.

As he thought about Joss, his anger mounted, knowing himself deceived. Oh, that one was Naomi's son, all right! Naomi meant trouble, always had. Trouble span round her like a centrifugal force, drawing in other people from the periphery. She had surely put Joss up to getting a job with Wilding's, to becoming friendly with Matthew. With the very obvious objective of getting into his good books before she dropped this bombshell.

The question was – aside from whether or not Joss was his son – what the devil was he going to do about it?

The blood pounded in his head.

He jumped when he heard the telephone ring. Few people knew his personal hotline number, which came straight through to him. Thinking it was Christine, he picked it up, an apology for his late arrival home on his lips. The apology died when he found he was talking to his old friend, Tom Callaghan.

Callaghan didn't waste words. 'I thought I should let you know that Naomi's back.'

'Well, thanks, but I've just been reading a letter from her, informing me of the fact.'

'This is bad news, isn't it?'

'Whenever has Naomi been anything else?'

'Does Nigel know?'

'I shouldn't think so. She particularly asked me not to tell him.'

There was a thoughtful pause at the other end of the line. 'I think he *should* know,' Callaghan said. 'If only for his own protection.'

Jake remembered then, something he ought not to have forgotten about Tom, and felt a moment of empathy with his friend, sensing the other's unremitting pain. And he knew that what Tom was really saying was something quite different.

Joss lounged in the chair, smoking, listening to the new CD he'd bought, with the volume turned up, all the windows open to the hot night, thinking, amongst other things, of Jake Wilding.

He'd been working for Jake for seven months now, an unprecedented time for Joss to stay with anything. His previous record had been six months when, with another man, he'd run a small waterfront restaurant in Honolulu. Mostly, it had been odd jobs whenever he found them around the world: a spell on a North Sea gas rig, a short time felling timber with the Forestry Commission in Scotland, three months as a short order cook in New York, and so on and so forth. In between, there had been countless other jobs, and rather a lot of activities best forgotten.

He had no more been to university and taken a degree in microbiology than pigs could fly. He'd lied his way round it to Jake when he wanted the job with Wilding's and Jake, taken with his open, frank and easy manner, had accepted what he wanted to hear.

Joss told lies as easily as he breathed. He'd been conditioned to it by the way he'd been brought up; lies had been a necessity by which he'd survived. He'd been fending for himself ever since he was fifteen. Snatched at six years old from his grandmother, whom he'd greatly loved, and swept unceremoniously off to Greece by a strange woman they said was his mother, treated with as much careless affection as a puppy and with much less discipline, he'd been allowed to go pretty much his own way, scraping up what education he could and learning, *en passant*, the laws of survival. Naomi had been a feckless mother, carelessly loving when she was reminded of her children by their presence and she was feeling well-disposed, forgetful of them when she was not. He was fifteen when he found the letter from England.

He'd picked it up when it arrived, and opened it before Naomi had had the chance to see it.

He'd always been curious about who his father was, until

that day when he'd seen what was written, and read the flamboyant signature. Jake, was all the signature said, but the letter had been written on headed business paper: Jake Wilding was a property developer and builder. And he was writing to ask Naomi for a divorce. It had already cost him a great deal of time and money to trace her, he wrote, but he was prepared to be generous if she would agree. She owed that to the boy.

Joss had read the letter with mounting excitement. He had a father, at last, his name was Jake Wilding, he lived in England. He had money. Joss had no feelings for this unknown father, but he had determined there and then to go to this place, Lavenstock, and seek him out, get what he could from him.

At fifteen, he was well able to pass for eighteen. He'd signed on with a merchant ship in Piraeus and would never have bothered to see his mother again if it hadn't been for Cassie. His only regret had been having to leave her behind. He loved his little sister as much as he was capable of loving anyone, and he wouldn't have left her if he hadn't known that her father's relatives, a fiercely possessive peasant family, would take care of her. She spent most of her time with them as it was. They adored her, tried to dress her like a little doll, which she hated, and spoiled her outrageously, which she tolerated. They would have liked to have adopted her legally but Naomi, out of some suddenly discovered maternal instinct, had stubbornly refused. She had let Cassie take the Andreas surname, but that was as far as she'd go.

Joss grinned now, to think that he had ever worried about Cassie, of all people.

His intention had been to make his way straight to England, but it hadn't been as easy as that. For a while, it was all he could do to survive. Later, when he'd learned the trick of it, other things had intervened and offered so much excitement that his original purpose had been driven to the back of his mind. His new life provided him with change and stimulus and the spice of danger and excitement he craved, the chance to prove he could live on his wits. From then on, he'd turned up on his mother's doorstep from time to time, when whatever he was doing brought him in her direction. The years passed, and he'd almost forgotten his original motive for leaving home when he heard about Naomi's legacy and her intention to move back to Lavenstock. The name had conjured up old memories, new possibilities, and he had arrived at the little house by the railway one night without warning and taken possession of the attic.

He'd then got himself a job at Wilding's. Naomi, though admitting that she had once known Jake, had said nothing to Joss about having been married to him, nor about him being Joss's father. And Joss didn't tell her what he knew. He concentrated on making a good impression on Jake before presenting him with a ready-made son. It was a pity there was now another son, Matthew, but Joss accepted this philosophically – lucky there was only one, and not several. It never occurred to him to ask who Matthew's mother was . . .

At that moment, Cassie came in. 'Turn that thing off, we're going to eat in the garden. I got a Chicken Chasseur at Marks and Spencer this afternoon – and a bottle of wine. You'd better come quick before she finishes it off. She's well away already.'

'Chicken Chasseur, eh? In the money, are we?'

Cassie grinned and tapped the side of her nose. 'Money? Don't be naive.'

You had to admire her.

No longer the baby sister he'd allowed to tag along after him, looked after with a fierce possessiveness, taught to swim, tucked up in bed, foraged for meals for when Naomi couldn't be bothered. Cassie was now a strong-minded young woman in her own right, stronger in some things, it amused him to admit, than he was, and equally unprincipled. Ruthless, in fact. Sometimes, she could frighten other people.

But not Joss. They were a pair. He smiled, stretched and stubbed out his cigarette before going out into the garden to join them, totally unprepared for the catastrophe waiting for him there. Together, they could do anything.

PART 2

October

6

Nigel Fontenoy, watching the Midland landscape flash past the carriage window, found himself in an increasingly bad temper. His return journey from London was being made intolerable by some yuppie using his mobile telephone as if he'd purchased a monopoly on personal space along with his first-class ticket. Nigel knew he ought to have protested but he was sure to be met by the sort of superciliousness he didn't feel he could cope with today – or any other day, truth to tell. He always avoided straight confrontations, preferring more devious methods of revenge.

Instead, like the other cowardly occupants of the carriage, he simply cast withering glances at the uncaring telephone user then turned to stare through the window as though the show-off conversations in the background had nothing to do with him, watching the grey skies and the trees bending to the wind and the autumn leaves flying.

Already October, and he only had until mid-November to make up his mind. He tried to concentrate on the terms which had been put forward at the meeting with Jermyn's. But his thoughts squirrelled around in his mind, refusing to be put into any sort of order. So much, of course, depended on his father, and he needed to be quite clear in his own mind what was entailed before presenting the idea to him. He was only *too* clear, he feared, as to what George's reactions would be. He was unlikely to agree to the proposition, at least in the first instance. It would be up to Nigel to put it to him in a favourable light. Ever since Jermyn's director, Alec Macaudle, had been to see the shop in September, Nigel had been trying to prepare the ground, but George seemed to have an uncanny knack of turning aside from the subject whenever it was raised. Occasionally, Nigel had received a distinct impression that George knew exactly what was going on, without having been told. It was possible. He was a wily old bird. On the other hand, how could he have found out, when Nigel had been at such pains to hide it from him? He couldn't surely have deduced it from that one visit Macaudle had made to the shop in September? George had hung around on that occasion, but Nigel had made sure of there being no opportunity to introduce them – and he'd had all subsequent correspondence addressed to him personally and had kept it securely locked up at all times.

George, however, was going to have to face the truth sooner or later. Provincial jewellers like Fontenoy's, however well-respected their name, were in the junior league nowadays . . . their outlets were narrow, competition was fierce. It wasn't as if they were London-based, working in the largest antique jewellery centre in the world. The only answer was to merge, to allow himself to be bought out by one of them: Jermyn's, to be precise. The shop would still be run by him, still be known as Cedar House Antiques, the only difference being that he would be relieved of the constant worry.

Meantime, though, he still had certain assets; the thought of one in particular went a very long way towards lightening the gloom. Yet he frowned, remembering the appointment that evening. It had been a long day, and he was tired, but he would need all his wits about him, all his powers of persuasion. He sat up straighter as they went through a tunnel and the reflection of a girl's face in the window from the next bank of seats sprang out – sweet, young, soft. Smiling. He returned the smile, knowing she could see his reflection, too. A good-looking man, well dressed, obviously prosperous, a mature man who knew how to charm women. The girl stopped smiling, stood up abruptly and left the compartment.

He shrugged. Forget it. In any case, he'd finished with all that now. He was becoming more circumspect as he grew older.

The appearance of the battered old railway buildings at the top of the embankment, just before the train plunged into the next tunnel, signalled it was time to collect his belongings and get ready for disembarking. Perhaps it was that young girl, or maybe a sudden memory of that unspeakable encounter last month, but at that moment the thought of Naomi slid again into his mind. Naomi at eighteen. A peculiar sort of excitement coursed through him. She might have changed with the years, but not so much that she wouldn't, considering her present circumstances, allow herself to be persuaded at last to see reason.

The weather had taken a turn for the worse as he came out of the station and headed for the car park. Rain was lashing down, it was distinctly chilly and a strong wind had got up. The biggest storm that Lavenstock had experienced for half a century, however, didn't begin in earnest until about ten, although it raged until dawn.

7

During the night, the Stockwell overflowed its banks, buildings were damaged, trees uprooted. At least one major accident was caused by a branch falling across a car windscreen, causing the driver to swerve and several vehicles to pile up behind him. An unlucky woman visitor, sleeping on a camp bed in a conservatory, was killed when a chimney-stack fell through the roof. On the outskirts of Lavenstock, an ancient tumbledown house, already dangerously shaky on its foundations, collapsed. The town had known nothing like it in living memory.

Old George Fontenoy, uneasy in his bed, was subliminally aware of the chaos outside, of the screech of the wind in the chimney and the rattling window-frames and the rain drumming on the roof, of bangs and crashes on the periphery of his drug-induced sleep. At some point the noise reached a crescendo that penetrated his subconscious and he awoke in panic and terror, his heart beating arrhythmically. Drenched in sweat, he lay listening to the cacophony outside, willing the sleeping pills to lull him back into oblivion. He didn't succeed for some time but later, much later, he did sleep.

Scarcely a soul in Lavenstock slept well that night.

Lindsay Hammond, home again for the weekend, lay rigid in her bed, trying to think of anything other than the gale . . . the new garden layout, for instance, which Christine had been trying to interest her in before bed. But thunder and lightning terrified her, and she couldn't concentrate her mind on Christine's ideas. She could only see the photos they'd been looking at, pictures of the original garden taken before the house was pulled down, showing a landscape of Victorian extremes: of threateningly spiky yuccas and downy grey Dusty Millers, poison-green spotted aucubas and feathery ferns, fleshy hellebores, deadly laburnum pods and gigantic, dangerous clumps of Japanese knotweed.

The wind was tearing through the wood, the branches soughing and creaking, and she imagined the creatures deep in the interior, the birds being blown from their nests, the little brown muntjak deer, trembling and terrified. But the house was new and kept in good repair, Jake had built well and strong. Nothing rattled, shook or fell off. She was glad she wasn't Cassie, alone with that grungy mother of hers in the horrid little house that looked as though it only needed a huff and a puff to blow it down.

She finally dropped off into an uneasy sleep, haunted by fantasies of the wind lifting Cassie's house up, whole, blowing it across the sky like some witch's hovel in one of her old fairy books. But even that wouldn't scare Cassie. She wasn't afraid of anything.

It was some time later that she awoke again as light flashed across her closed curtains. The house had been struck by lightning, she thought in panic, then realized it was only the headlights of a car.

Cassie Andreas certainly wasn't frightened by the storm but she found it hard to calm down and get to sleep. Storms excited her – and she was far too hyped-up, wide awake, listening to the creaking and groaning of the loose section of guttering outside her bedroom window and the intermittent banging of the side gate, which had lost its fastening. She thought about getting up again and making herself some hot chocolate, but she'd only just got warm and at the thought of leaving her duvet-wrapped snugness she stayed put.

The storm reminded her of the *meltemi*. When she'd been staying with her Greek grandmother, she could pretend to be afraid and creep into her bed and snuggle up to her vast, pillowy softness. But this was England, she was no longer a child, there was no grandmother here, and nobody could imagine snuggling up to Naomi for comfort.

She was glad she'd allowed her mother to come here. She could have persuaded her not to, you could talk Naomi into anything, and Cassie had early discovered she could manipulate anyone, if she chose. She was sorry to have left the sun behind, but here she and Joss had rich friends – Lindsay and, of course, Matthew. Money was of paramount importance to Cassie, her life so far having been singularly lacking in it. Also, in Greece she'd always felt herself to be some sort of hybrid, neither Greek nor English. She'd hated that, sensing that there must be something better than either the dull, peasant life of her Greek relatives or the feckless, hand-to-mouth, come-day go-day existence of her mother.

'We'll see about staying here, it all depends,' her mother had said when they arrived.

Yes, we'll see, thought Cassie, now, with a secret smile. We shall see.

The gate banged loudly again, several times in quick, erratic succession. She wondered if the roof might blow off, which in this house seemed entirely possible. The broken-down fence would certainly be laid low. Perhaps Joss might now be shamed into doing something about it, he was competent enough, though whenever he was asked to do anything like that he always managed to find urgent business elsewhere. If it had to be fixed, she would have to do it herself, as usual. She was the only one who ever did things around here. She wished, passionately, that she'd been the son, and Joss the daughter. She often thought of herself as a boy.

Cassie wondered how Joss had been able to go on working for Jake Wilding for so long. She didn't think Jake was the sort to tolerate slacking and incompetence.

'No problem,' Joss had said, with his slow smile, when she'd asked him once. 'I'm the blue-eyed boy as far as Jake's concerned.'

Cassie, however, had known men like Jake in the village at home. 'All smiles to your face and a dagger in the back when you're not looking,' she'd said darkly, though the real reason she didn't like Jake was because she knew he instinctively distrusted her. She smiled, amused by the idea, and not at all upset.

But then a little worm of fear began to burrow beneath Cassie's hard little shell. She tried to ignore it, but a web had been woven, meshing them all together into a tight knot, from which none of them might find it easy to extricate themselves.

Joss, unable to wind down either, was smoking in bed, his thoughts jumping back to that September evening when Cassie had called him into the garden to eat.

It came to him in a series of images, sharp and clear: the scruffy old table with the wonky leg which stood under the three arthritic old apple trees. Its grey weathered graininess and the stains of countless bird-droppings. The empty plates on the table, cleared of the illicit Chicken Chasseur. And the wine bottle, Naomi's glass. Cassie, lying on her stomach in the grass, her chin propped up on her hand, her eyes black and shining, exhilarated by the Wagnerian *Sturm und Drang* issuing from her radio. The end of a sweltering day and the dusk giving the garden an illusion of tranquillity. The scent of apples and, barely visible in the dusk, some woody Michaelmas daisies, bleached of colour by neglected old age and the half-light, reflecting the white blur of Naomi's face as she leaned over to pick up her glass.

He'd seen that she was worried about something, or as worried as Naomi ever could be, and that in itself gave significance to the moment. It couldn't have been the bills which were piling up, for she simply tossed them aside, nor the repairs the house needed – she knew all about these things, and that retribution was only a step away, but let them slide off her consciousness like water off a duck's back. He knew this was something a good deal more fundamental.

A few minutes before, Cassie had been clearing windfalls to make a space to lie on the grass, examining the apples for worms or wasps and putting the best to one side, suggesting, without much hope, that they could be made into a pie. Apple pies, unknown in Greece, were just another part of the British way of life that Cassie had embraced with such fervour.

She hadn't wanted to come here originally, but it was obvious that she was now in her element. She loved the English countryside, its green lushness; grey English cities, strawberries and cream, ready-sliced bread for toast, and even the soft English rain. This year, there had actually been sun. She was well on the way to becoming a born-again Anglophile.

Now, at the mention of apple pies, Naomi was rolling her eyes as if she'd never heard of such a thing. 'What ideas you do get! You pick them up and make one if you want one so much.'

'All right, I will!'

Naomi laughed and Joss had been furious with her. He lounged back in one of the old-fashioned deck chairs they'd found in the outhouse and put his feet up on the table, to annoy her. She didn't even notice.

Cassie glared at Naomi, too, and turned the Valkyries off mid-ride, with a snap that nearly broke the switch. She was strong willed and quick to anger, and she could have no idea how to set about making apple pies, but he knew she'd find out. She had a tenacity he envied. If she was determined to do something, she'd do it, come hell or high water. He and Cassie, separated by eight years, had come from the same mould, but her anger was quick and violent, whereas his was a slow burn.

As if what he'd been thinking about inside the house had transmitted itself to her, Naomi, her tongue loosened with alcohol, had unexpectedly broached the subject of his working for Jake Wilding. 'I wish you two weren't so involved with the Wildings, with Jake and Matthew.' She watched Cassie under her eyelids.

'Why? Does it matter?' Joss had asked, lazily, trying not to let her know that she had the whole of his attention. She had Cassie's too, he could tell from her sudden tense stillness. Naomi took a deep breath and then in a rush, she told him it mattered very much, because she had once not only known Jake Wilding, she had been married to him.

'Right,' he said, draining his wine.

There was silence. 'You knew,' she said. 'Who told you?'

'I've known since I was fifteen.' He watched for her reaction as he told her about opening that letter from England.

'Joss!' She wasn't shocked, hardly surprised; amused, in fact, a small smile touching the corners of her mouth. 'Opening my letters! That was never one of your most endearing traits. You were bound to find out something disagreeable sooner or later.'

He'd allowed the silence to lengthen, and felt rage tightening his skull. She'd known. She, his mother, had known all along what he was doing and had never tried to stop him. Both he and Cassie had opened their mother's mail since they could first read, just as they'd helped themselves to money from her purse, or from odd amounts left lying around, by her or anyone else. They'd become adept at steaming envelopes open and sealing them up again unnoticeably, enough to fool Naomi, at any rate, though it usually wasn't worth the effort they put into it. Mothers were supposed to stop you doing things like that – yet she'd known and never even tried to show him that it was an activity that was to say the least socially undesirable. She'd let him carry on doing it, simply because she was too lazy, or too uncaring, to stop it. She'd probably known about the pilferings from her purse, too. Sometimes he felt like killing his mother.

'Is it so "disagreeable" that I'm Jake Wilding's son, then?' he'd asked, when he could speak. He tried to read her face, moon-pale in the dusk, but he was too far away to see her expression. 'He talked about me in the letter – the boy, he called me. Didn't he even know my name?' He couldn't keep the bitterness out of his voice and he heard her catch her breath.

By this time, Naomi had drunk most of the wine. She poured the dregs into her glass. A train came out of the tunnel and thundered past. The tree branches bent and several more apples fell to join the others on the grass. The fence above the embankment swayed, the glasses and bottle rattled on the table. 'I hate this house,' she said.

'Never mind the house, it serves its purpose. What about my question?'

Ignoring him, she went on in a dreamy voice, 'My grandfather was a stationmaster, that was how he came to live here. Later, my father bought the house, and my mother kept it, even after she remarried.'

'Will you answer me? I want to *know*.'

'What you both should know,' she said, 'is that the boy Jake referred to in that letter was Matthew. Matthew is my son.'

Whether you believed Naomi or not was largely a function of how young, or how credulous you were. As a child, he'd believed her stories implicitly, until he'd learned scepticism. But that hot September night, after the first initial shock, he'd had no difficulty whatsoever in believing what she said as, word by shattering word, she proceeded to demolish all his previously conceived ideas.

When she'd finished and he was at last able to breathe again, he'd met Cassie's eyes. The tension that was always there between them sparked like two bare wires meeting. They had understood each other perfectly.

On the morning after the storm, George Fontenoy awoke to an awareness of calamity, to an undefined feeling of trouble. Specifically, that something was wrong about the light filtering through the curtains. He could hear rain still lashing down as he got out of bed, walked stiffly to the window and drew the curtains on to a scene of carnage.

The old cedar of Lebanon had finally succumbed. It lay across the length of the garden, just missing the house but almost obliterating everything else. It had, after all, been a mighty tree, nearly two hundred feet high and with a spread of fifty feet. The robinia had gone down with it, and the old magnolia, and it had flattened the massive spread of rhododendrons and the laurel hedge separating the garden from its neighbour. The difference was astonishing. The abundance of light, the excess of space created a new world. A double-decker bus cruised surrealistically past in the previously hidden road behind the garden wall. On the top deck people were staring and pointing out the fallen tree to each other. The cedar had been a well-loved landmark in Lavenstock, so much so that when workmen had arrived to lop overhanging branches which were said to be obscuring road signs, an immediate outcry had prevented them. Instead, it was the road signs which were moved.

The tree was known to have been at least two hundred years old, as old as the house itself, at a guess. George had climbed it as a boy, gathered its fragrant cones for winter fires and to gild for Christmas decorations; his mother had wheeled a trolley out for tea beneath its spreading branches on summer afternoons. As a baby, he'd slept in his pram under its shade and, in their turn, his children. His wife, Margaret, had set up her easel and painted the house from there.

Lightning was not supposed to strike in the same place twice but the cedar had been struck three times to his certain knowledge, each time damaging it and weakening its structure further. The last attack had been in the previous year, when one of its three massive limbs had been lost and the lightning had corkscrewed down the trunk, through the roots and into the earth, leaving great red weals in its bark which had wept for weeks.

He too wept a little now, unashamedly, mourning the cedar and many other things besides, then braced himself to face the day. But the calamitous death of the tree wasn't, by a very long chalk, the worst of it. There would be more to weep over before long.

8

The two detectives stood in the cordoned-off alley in the pouring rain, she with her raincoat collar pulled up and a sou'wester jammed over her hair, he towering over her with the hood of his waterproof well down over his long, lugubrious face. The area had been taped off, a yellow tent covered the place where the body had lain, a police constable stood on guard to ward off the curious, though there was nothing to be seen.

It wasn't unusual for the police to make a pick-up in Nailers' Yard. Drunk, drugged or homeless – occasionally dead. But it was unheard of, shocking and somehow faintly reprehensible for a man like that to have been found there in the small hours of a wild night, bleeding to death in a dirty puddle among the overturned dustbins and other debris that had been whirled into the cul-de-sac on Force 9 gusts. He'd been knifed and was in a bad way and, though he had immediately been taken to the County Hospital, he'd died before he could be put into intensive care.

When one of the constables on patrol, diving for cover into the Rose's doorway, had literally stumbled over him, the alley had been mysteriously free of any of its regulars, the usual shapeless bundles huddled into cardboard boxes. The storm could have accounted for it. Be that as it may, anyone who might have witnessed the deed had long since departed elsewhere.

There was nothing to identify the body. His wallet had disappeared along with his attacker, but a sharp-eyed nurse at the hospital had recognized him as he was later being prepared for the mortuary. He was Nigel Fontenoy, owner of Cedar House Antiques. Locally well-known, in his mid-forties, unmarried, said to be a fastidious and cultured man.

'So what was he doing in Nailers' Yard?' Abigail Moon asked, a rhetorical question because the end of the passage had long been bricked up. There was wasteland beyond, but the yard itself now led nowhere except to the side entrance of the Rose.

Carmody raised a cynical eyebrow. Fontenoy wouldn't have been the first to find his way to the side door and up to the private rooms, though he might well have been the first to come out alone.

'Nobody's admitting to seeing him in there if he was. Cellini says there was only himself and two of his girls upstairs all last night. He shut early because of the weather. Says he doesn't know Fontenoy but he would say that, wouldn't he? Avoiding trouble's second nature to our Sal.' He swiped water from the end of his nose. 'Bloody rain.'

The rain had been the killer's biggest ally. Getting the injured man to hospital had been a first priority; by the time the Scenes of Crime team had arrived, traces of any struggle that might have taken place had been obliterated. It was still raining in a steady downpour, though the gale had blown itself out, leaving the town to lick its wounds and assess the damage. Carmody looked without enthusiasm at the mess of stinking dustbin contents, fish and chip papers, burger boxes and worse, blown into a drift against the end wall, all of which would have to be meticulously picked over by the luckless search team.

Nailers' Yard, older than the nightclub it flanked by several hundred years, had seen plenty of violence in its time. An inn had once occupied the place where the Rose now stood, having bequeathed to the club only its name. Iron nails had once been forged in the nail shops behind the hovels at the end of the yard where the nailers had lived. A rough, drunken lot they'd been, fighting drunk by Saturday night, spoiling for a punch-up with the local colliers, who were drunk all the time. There were no nailers now, no colliers, but nothing else much had changed in three or four hundred years. Yet the past couldn't be ignored. The man who'd been stabbed had had a past, which may have contributed towards his death.

Abigail said, 'The weapon?'

'No sight of it yet. Doubt if there will be. The river's too handy.'

'Organize a search for it, Ted, all the same.'

The side door of the Rose opened and they watched Cellini approach: a short, stout individual whose sallow complexion was not appreciably improved by the light filtering through a green and yellow striped golf umbrella.

'You in charge here?' he demanded of Carmody in a broad Brummie accent. There was little left of Salvatore Cellini's Italian origins now except his name, his curly black hair and his big, dark, oh-so-innocent eyes.

'No, Inspector Moon here is,' Carmody said as Abigail held out her hand. 'I'm Sergeant Carmody.'

The nightclub owner looked taken aback. 'Where's Mayo, then? Job of this sort not important enough for him?'

'Never mind that. And you mind your Ps and Qs, Sal. Detective Chief Inspector Mayo to you,' Carmody answered. 'And we're asking the questions, so likewise.'

It made a change from domestic violence, thought Abigail. Which was what had been occupying her latterly, until her recent promotion. A highly stressful job, involving the sordid and messy results of mostly marital discord, but it was better than one of the safe backroom jobs all too often allocated to women. Or so she'd imagined, until picking up the pieces of shattered lives, and not always being able to put them together again, had somewhat altered her ideas.

'Well, if you're in charge here, *Inspector* Moon, I'd very much appreciate it if you'd get them goons off of my premises,' Cellini grumbled, indicating the odd police bods hanging around. 'They won't find nothing – you ask me, they're just looking for excuses to get out of the rain and drink my coffee.'

Abigail didn't blame them. She could have used a cup of hot coffee herself, her hands and feet were frozen. She looked at her watch. She had to report back to Mayo and had the PM to attend in an hour and could well push off and leave the rest of this to Carmody, grabbing a coffee at the station on the way. He was unflappable and reliable, and experienced enough after more than twenty years with the police in Liverpool to cope with a simple mugging. If it was simple.

Of course it was. It would be a big mistake, just because this was the first actual murder she'd encountered in her new capacity (although some incidents had already come perilously close to it) to blow up this run-of-the-mill mugging out of proportion. But intuition told her it wasn't as straight-forward as that. If Fontenoy hadn't been in the nightclub, then what had he been doing in Nailers' Yard? What had he been doing out at all, come to that, on a night like last night? Without even a coat?

He'd been left for dead by whoever had stabbed him, but he hadn't been, not quite. Had the constable stumbled over him earlier, he might still be alive. An amateur killer then, and if not a mugger, then one who had taken some trouble to remove anything personal from the body. But why? Identification would have been delayed, but not for long. Fontenoy would soon have been missed. But whether it was a mugging gone wrong or not, the result was still murder.

The question of what Mayo would do in the circumstances crossed her mind, but she didn't let it stay there. She dis-approved of this retrograde kind of thinking. She was still responsible to him, however, and since he'd been largely instrumental in recommending her for this latest move up the ladder, seeing to it she was in the right place at the right time, she felt on her mettle not to make a hash of it. Besides, he was in no mood to tolerate incompetence at the moment. It was rumoured that he, too, was in for a promotion, though if true it wasn't doing his temper much good. She suspected there were reasons for that. Something of his private life was known to her, since she and Sergeant Alex Jones had become friends – Alex, who'd been injured in a shoot-out at a petrol station and was now on extended sick leave. Meeting death at close quarters concentrated the mind wonderfully and she was, Abigail knew, seriously questioning her future. Abigail had her own thoughts on how things might turn out, but only time would prove whether she was right or not.

'I'm not happy about this, Ted,' she murmured in an aside to Carmody, and to Cellini, 'I'd like a few words with you myself, if you don't mind.'

With an excessive show of holding on to his patience, the nightclub owner led the way in through the side door and into a small vestibule, off which a door opened into the main part of the premises. The club's front entrance was all black glass and chrome, a thirties decor with a glittering bar behind it, a couple of roulette tables, a square of parquet for shuffling around on and a minute stage draped with black velvet curtains artistically appliquéd with a couple of dancing nudes in eau-de-Nil satin and diamanté. All right, if that sort of thing turned you on. The whine of the vacuum cleaner could be heard coming from this part of the club. Cellini hesitated, eventually waving them towards the floor above, which offered none of the downstairs attractions, only a steep, narrow staircase and an indifferently decorated room at the top with a small corner bar, a few tables and chairs. The punters didn't come up here to look at the decorations.

Once there, Cellini changed tactics. His truculent expression was replaced by one meant to be ingratiating. 'How about a drop o' summat as'll warm yer up, and I don't mean coffee?' His accent had grown even thicker. He smiled and looked sinister.

Carmody said, 'Coffee'll do fine, ta.'

Abigail divested herself of her dripping mac and pulled off her rain hat, freeing her thick, wavy bronze hair, recently cut and still feeling strange. She'd needed to mark her new authority with some kind of statement, but couldn't bring herself to go the whole hog, so it still wasn't very short. She was aware of Cellini's eyes on her even as he pushed open a door behind the bar and shouted over his shoulder for three coffees, automatically assessing the length of her legs, the size of her bra cup. She said coldly, 'Tell us what happened last night.'

'Nothing happened, and I mean that, worse luck. Scheduled to be a big night, it was. I'd booked a male stripper – not what you might call a draw for most of our gentlemen customers, still, you have to cater for the fair sex nowadays, know what I mean? But apart from a couple of hen parties that left early we didn't get any women in, neither. Dead loss, it was. Buggered things up every which way, in fact, the weather last night, pardon my French, Inspector. Packed it in by eleven and shut up shop.'

'What about up here?' Carmody asked.

'Same applies. Anybody comes up here, he's been invited, and there wasn't nobody to invite, was there, Tammy?'

'Like the grave it was,' agreed Tammy, a Dolly Parton blonde well past her sell-by date, wearing skin-tight jeans and white stilettos and a sweater cut low enough to cause serious concern when she joined them, propping her elbows on the table and leaning over the steaming cups of cappuccino.

'Special customers up here, Sal?' asked Carmody.

Cellini didn't bat an eyelid. 'That's right. Regulars. Them as likes a quiet drink.'

Abigail said, 'Was Mr Fontenoy one of them?'

'Never clapped eyes on him. Never set foot in the Rose, he didn't.'

'Maybe he came in when you weren't here?'

'I'm *always* here. I don't leave my business to nobody else.'

Sal Cellini was the sort who lied even when it wasn't necessary, out of habit, but in this case Abigail believed him. He'd come a long way by devious means, and wasn't about to queer his own pitch. He wasn't that stupid. In his way, he was to be admired. He knew the police had a very good idea what he was up to but he was careful not to stray outside the boundaries of what was admissible – a little gambling, no drinking under age, no sex, at least not on the premises. If his girls made themselves available to his clients off the premises that was their own affair; it was unlikely they'd admit to Cellini taking a cut from their immoral earnings.

Tammy, when questioned, said she'd left the club at just after eleven, in company with the other hostess, Debbie, a girl with whom she shared a flat around the corner. She was prepared to swear there'd been no one at all lying around in the alley when they left.

'Sure? 'Course I'm sure! Couldn't hardly help being sure,

could we? Any of that lot are around, you're lucky if you get past with nothing worse than a hand up your skirt!'

Abigail drove back to Milford Road Police Station, assessing her chances of being kept on this case. As a newly made up DI, she was hopeful: she'd acquitted herself well when, as a sergeant, she had last worked on a murder inquiry with Mayo. And at the moment, he was hard-pressed.

Things might just be in her favour.

9

Detective Chief Inspector Gil Mayo was an energetic York-
shireman in his early forties, a big man with dark hair and
searching, dark grey eyes. Sometimes on a short fuse, sometimes incommunicative, inclined to be intimidating, especially with those on the wrong side of the law or those who'd
tried to pull a fast one and had reason to fear his wrath. He
expected – and got – more from his officers than they
thought they were capable of giving. Willingly, to their
surprise.

He watched Abigail carefully while she outlined what had
gone on so far, while mentally surveying the resources he
had available. The picture, as ever, was not encouraging. He
himself was up to his ears, with at least half a dozen overlap-
ping cases, one of them involving the prosecution of the
armed robbers of a post office, an incident which had already
led to one murder and might turn out to be a double one if
the second victim died. He had no other DI available. Atkins
was on the sick list and Kite, the sergeant who was like
his right arm, had been seconded to a working party on
the setting up of drug surveillance teams. In addition the
super, Howard Cherry, was currently absent at a high-level
conference and a good part of his workload had devolved
upon Mayo. He needed someone experienced in this sort of
investigation, and wondered whether to ask for someone
from outside the division to help out, well aware of what
Abigail Moon was hoping for.

He recognized her ambition, having enough of it himself
to be causing problems at the moment – decisions to make,
weighing the disadvantages of promotion, of becoming a

71

strategy man and all that went with it, against remaining a hands-on copper. Politics also came into it – you couldn't go on refusing promotion for ever, your motives became suspect, as though you were aware that you'd reached the limits of your own competence. And when it got to that stage, those who counted soon began to believe it was true.

He'd reason enough to feel that everything could be going for him, and yet his life was on a see-saw, professionally on the upside, personally right at the bottom. About as far down there as you could possibly go, his future with Alex being uncertain, to say the least. He did his best not to dwell on it. But last night, driving home and climbing the stairs to his empty flat he'd found himself doing just that, like probing a sore tooth.

He was alone in the flat with only the ticking of his old clocks and Bert for company. His daughter Julie had settled herself in Australia, with no sign of wanting to return in the foreseeable future, and he missed her. Independence was something he'd encouraged in her, then found he didn't much like the form it had taken. As for Alex . . . funny that he should feel her absence here so keenly – she had her own flat, had steadfastly refused to move in with him. He was slowly learning that he might have to accept the situation as it stood. To press her too hard into making that total commitment he himself wanted might be to lose her altogether.

At any rate, nobody could say Bert wasn't pleased to see him. Mayo scratched the parrot's gaudy head as he dished out his food. Very choosy about his food, Bert, picking out the choicest seed from his mixture and disdainfully discarding the rest on to the floor around his cage.

'At least there's somebody alive when I come in at night, mate,' Mayo told him. Self-pity wasn't something he encouraged in himself as a rule, and Bert very properly responded with a sharp nip to his finger. He was a bird who vocally craved affection but liked to remind people of his independence.

There had been a postcard from Alex, wedged in between his gas bill and an offer of a timeshare in Portugal. She was enjoying the convalescent holiday with her sister Lois in Devon, the food was good, they'd been walking every day, healthwise she felt back to normal. She didn't say 'Wish you were here'.

And, since it was only a postcard, there was naturally no mention of whether she'd finalized her decision to quit the police.

'Leaving the force? You're giving up your *career*, for God's sake!' he'd said, winded, when she'd thrown that one at him.

'It's gone sour on me.'

'We all get disillusioned from time to time. And this has been a particularly bad time for you.' For both of them . . . So bad, when her life had hung in the balance, that he came out in a cold sweat even now, just thinking about it. A bad time, yes, but lit by moments of unexpected joy, that she was alive, and would be well.

'It's not a passing thing, Gil. All this has nothing to do with it. I've thought about it for months. I'm just not dedicated enough, not like Abigail Moon, for instance.' She'd added, 'It'll solve a lot of other problems, too,' and he'd stopped himself from saying that could be altered at any time, because this was a cul-de-sac they'd been down more times than he could remember. Their relationship was a complex one.

It wasn't just that she didn't want to marry him, she didn't want to marry anyone, if it would get in the way of her career. And if he detected in that the hand of her sister Lois, who had a poor opinion of men and of Gil Mayo in particular, he'd managed to stop himself from saying so. So where had all the dreams gone?

Abigail, then Sergeant, now Inspector Moon, sitting before him with the light of ambition in her green eyes, was a very different kettle of fish. A graduate entrant, she was marked out for a quick sprint up the ladder. Tough, although not half as tough as she thought herself. Competent and smart but, like all these high-flyers, long on theory, short on experience, though that, he acknowledged, was hardly their fault: coming up through the ranks so quickly, they didn't have the chance to get it. To compensate, she had the ability to operate on personal initiative, the willingness to accept responsibility, the nous to know how far she could cope, the grace to admit it when she couldn't.

He drummed his fingers on the desk as he thought. His first skimming over of the facts had told him this was quite likely to be an everyday, common-or-garden mugging but now, something about Abigail's swift summing-up was telling him otherwise. He'd learned to trust her quick intuition which, coupled with his own experience, told him this might turn out to be a major homicide investigation, and one which was ultimately his responsibility.

'All right, stay with it, Abigail. I shall be tied up in court for most of today and possibly tomorrow, so it looks as though you're going to be lumbered with the PM and the rest. I'll leave you to it, but let me know how you go on.'

He was already shuffling papers together, his mind on the next thing. As she rose to go, he said, almost as an after-thought, 'I'll be glad to have you working with me.' It was, however, said with one of his rare smiles. Seeing what it did for him, how attractive it made him appear, Abigail thought it was a pity he didn't smile more often.

'Thank you, sir.'

She was happy enough with what she'd got, realizing it was as far as he could go, considering her lack of experience in this direction, and more generous than she'd expected. She tried not to let it show, but she felt like a cat that had got a taste of the cream as she left Mayo's office.

She barely had time to burn her tongue with machine coffee from a styrofoam cup before starting out, though if she'd missed the PM altogether, it wouldn't have made an unstoppable gap in her life – post mortems being top of her list of things she could do without. She tried bracing admon-itions to herself – Come on, Abigail, you've been here before! – and more in similar vein, as she drove across to the mor-tuary. For however stomach-churning it might be, whatever she might feel at the waste and ultimate stupidity, the barbar-ousness of murder, she needed to see the body of Nigel Fon-tenoy. To try and begin to know what sort of person he had been, that someone had felt the need to deprive him of his right to live. In the event, she was glad she'd made it, for several reasons.

'Forceful stab wound to the abdomen, penetrating the abdominal aorta,' the rubicund pathologist announced with his usual cheerful insouciance, a tape recorder switched on as he worked. 'So he wouldn't have lasted long. There'd be blood, yes, but probably not as much as you'd expect – the haemorrhage was mostly internal. He'd be dead within a couple of hours, most likely, which makes it – say, somewhere around midnight?'

'What sort of weapon?'

'Mm, needs thinking about, that. Slender, tapering, with a very sharp point, lozenge-shaped in cross-section.'

'Any idea what it might be?'

'The depth of penetration indicates a length of about six inches . . . Think of a small stiletto, but thinner. Probably employed by a right-handed person striking downwards. A single entry wound, at an angle from the left, slightly off-centre, and corresponding cuts on the clothing – one through his shirt where the weapon entered and two others through his tie. Nice one, by the way, he had good taste . . . Wonder where he bought it? But those cuts, measuring from where the tie was knotted, were a couple of inches above the entry wound. Which would suggest – ?'

'That he was sitting down or leaning over when he was attacked?' Abigail supplied dutifully.

'Good girl!' Timpson-Ludgate cast his beaming approbation over her. He only just failed to pat her on the head. 'Yes, the position of the body when seated, especially if slumped, or leaning forward, would have meant that his tie was probably hanging over his waistband as the knife went through it.'

Sitting down, relaxed, shirt sleeves rolled up, no jacket, facing his attacker? Not much of a struggle? So, like most murder victims, Nigel Fontenoy had probably known his killer, ruling out the opportunist mugging theory, and the possibility that the attack had taken place in Nailers' Yard.

'You'll see the body's been subject to a fair bit of man-handling,' Timpson-Ludgate went on. 'If you look at the drag-marks on the backs of his shoes where they've scraped the ground, and the bump on the back of his head. These abrasions on his nose and chin suggest he was pulled face downwards at one time, from the gravel embedded in the grazes.'

'Could a woman have done it – got him in and out of a vehicle?'

'With extreme difficulty, unless she was an Olympic weightlifter. Your average woman might have been able to drag him out, but getting him in would've been a different matter. He's a big chap, six-two and well-built with it.'

So he'd been moved from the scene of the crime, but why leave him where he would so quickly be found? And identified without too much difficulty? It wasn't easy to conceal a body, not permanently, but here there'd been no attempt. It had been a stinking night, though. The sort of weather to thwart even carefully laid plans, with power lines down, roads blocked with fallen debris. A panic attempt to get rid of the body? Common sense was telling Abigail that was how it might have been.

The clothes he'd been wearing, soaked with rain and in a polythene bag ready to be gently dried out in the lab, had been good. Charcoal-grey trousers with a faint blue pin-stripe, a self-striped silk shirt in pale grey. The tie Timpson-Ludgate had admired was a designer one patterned in blues and greens on dark grey, now patched with blood. Classy shoes and silk socks. The body had well-shaped hands, large with manicured nails, and an ink stain near the tip of the right middle finger. He'd kept himself in good condition, but his face, without the animation of life, said nothing except that he'd been a handsome guy with a firm chin, smooth-skinned and no slackness, going slightly bald at the front.

Attractive to women, she suspected. The sort of man she'd have found attractive herself, maybe, if looks were all that mattered, with the sort of face you remembered.

10

After stopping off at the station to make several phone calls, to arrange for the Scenes of Crime team to be sent to Nigel Fontenoy's home, and to leave a brief note of the PM findings for Mayo as she consumed a hasty sandwich, Abigail drove across to Cedar House Antiques, drawing in behind Carmody's car. Other police vehicles were already there, and a uniformed PC stationed by the shop door.

The shop itself was part of a large stuccoed house at the corner of two intersecting roads just off the town centre, one of a pair at each end of a still elegant terrace of smaller Georgian houses, all with their own gardens stretching out in front. Some of the houses had now been turned into offices for architects, solicitors and the like, and emulsioned in pale Georgian colours. Painted a standard white, the Cedar House looked naked and less impressive than it had appeared when partly screened by the spreading dark green branches of the old tree. The discreet sign fixed to the wall – 'Cedar House Antiques' – on the other hand, was far more visible.

She stopped for a moment to join the crowd gaping at the stricken tree, its roots indecently exposed, like a drunken woman showing her underwear. The rain had stopped and the damp air was resinous, reminiscent of Christmas trees. A photographer from the *Advertiser* was taking pictures for the next edition, looking round for a photogenic victim to pose against the tree's exposed root ball and demonstrate its awesome size. His eye fell on Abigail. She moved quickly before he could make the suggestion and tried to dodge a reporter from the same paper hanging hopefully around the double gates at the side. True to form, having got wind of something more dramatic than a fallen tree, they were already starting to sniff hopefully around. Cedar House Antiques was going to feature prominently in the local news this week, one way or another.

'Go home,' she said, waving her hand as he approached her, 'we shan't be giving any more statements yet.' A press release had been issued, but had merely named the victim of a suspected mugging as Nigel Fontenoy, coupled with the usual routine appeal for information.

The reporter had recognized her. 'Don't be like that, Inspector Moon! Your gaffer's just gone and I must say he was a bit more accommodating.'

'Then you won't want anything more from me.'

Been and gone already, had he, while she was at the PM? This was Mayo's idea of leaving her to it, she thought, disgruntled, but in no position to throw her weight around. She was satisfied that she'd set most of the necessary procedures in motion, and Carmody would've covered the rest. Good old Carmody. Reliable and steady, he'd never set the Thames on fire, but he'd never stand by and watch it burn, either. He'd have dealt with the usual grumbles about all the leg work that would have to be done, all the hours of foot slogging, knowing how bored the troops would be with having to ask the same questions while paying careful attention to predictable answers in case one of them contained a nugget of gold. And he'd know they were token grumbles because this was how it was, and anyway, there was consolation in the form of hours of overtime.

'The press are outside; what's Mayo told them?' she asked the sergeant, who was talking to two DCs: the tall, handsome Farrar, and young, curly-haired Jenny Platt, in a back room which held a large impregnable-looking safe, a bank of cupboards, a long deal table and some filing cabinets.

'Summat and nowt,' Carmody said, torturing his Scouse into a fair imitation of Mayo's Yorkshire accent. 'You know the gaffer. Just enough to keep 'em out of our hair for a bit. Forensics are here.'

'Didn't take them long.' Mollified, Abigail took stock. Beyond this room she could see through an open door into a kitchen of sorts, equipped with a gas water-heater above an old-fashioned sink and a cooker of ancient vintage.

'That's just used for making coffee and so on,' Farrar informed her. 'There's a proper kitchen in the main house where Fontenoy lived with his father. The old man's there now with his nephew.'

'How's he taking it?'

'Confused. I'd almost say he was more concerned about the tree if I didn't think it was shock. It takes some people like that, you know, shock. That's what I was telling the Sarge when you –'

'Yeah,' Carmody said, 'you were.' Farrar was famous for it, teaching his grandmother to suck eggs. It wasn't an endearing trait.

'Has he said where Nigel was last night?' Abigail asked the DC. Though he constantly irritated her, she sometimes felt sorry for him. His sights were set on being chief constable or maybe, at a pinch, he'd settle for chief super. He was keen, able, willing to work hard – and, despite having passed his sergeant's exams, getting nowhere fast, poor devil, because there were fifty applicants for every ten vacancies and his face and his manner didn't fit.

He was unabashed. 'Fontenoy was working down here in the office to get their new catalogue finished, but apparently he rarely went to bed before the small hours. The old man swears he never would have gone out without telling him.'

'Don't suppose he heard anything?'

'He takes sleeping pills but he woke about midnight – thinks it must have been the tree going down that woke him, but he managed to get off again. The neighbours say the tree didn't fall until about four this morning, though, so it may have been Nigel going out that woke him.'

'Being taken out, more probably. It's unlikely he was stabbed where he was found – here, ten to one – as you must've gathered when the SOCOs arrived.' Quickly, she summarized what the pathologist had said.

'No obvious signs,' said Carmody.

'Forensics'll say for sure.' She looked assessingly at the spartan surroundings. 'This surely isn't the office?'

'Only the back one, where they keep stores and so on. The main office is glassed in at the back of the shop,' Farrar offered, opening the door into the short passage which led into the shop to let Abigail and Carmody pass through ahead of him.

'OK, Keith, thanks, no need to come with us. The fewer feetmark the better.'

'Ma'am,' said the DC stiffly. She threw him a look over her shoulder but he had closed the door before she could see his expression and hopefully before he heard the distinctly uncomplimentary remark she muttered under her breath. Farrar's shenanigans she could do without. It wasn't her fault Ted Carmody had been brought in from outside as her sergeant rather than Farrar having been made up. Not Carmody's fault either.

Behind the door, Jenny Platt was thinking the same thing. 'Leave it out, Jen!' Farrar said sourly, correctly interpreting the look she gave him.

'Oh, touchy!'

In this respect, Farrar was. But this time he let it pass. He was learning, slowly, that there were times to keep his tongue between his teeth.

Nobody ever said it was easy, Jenny thought, but some of us manage it. She kept herself going by a firm belief that she'd get there one day. Not as fast or as far as Moon, who'd done well, even by male standards, but then, Jenny wasn't on accelerated promotion, she'd never been to university. Bright enough, if she'd wanted to, but not as single-minded as Abigail Moon. She'd opted for a practical approach and a less meteoric rise, and a bit of fun in between, and so far hadn't regretted the decision.

Donning the mandatory white overalls, Abigail and the sergeant entered the shop, which was swarming with similarly clad white figures, busy with video cameras, vacuum cleaners, rolls of Sellotape, making their meticulous and exhaustive examination, working from the doorway inwards.

An access path to the small glassed-in office had been delineated with white tape. 'Don't go in there yet, we haven't got to it,' warned Sergeant Dexter, in charge of the SOCO team, and He-who-must-be-obeyed. Abigail had to make do with peering through the doorway. The desk, an ornate affair in Chippendale-style mahogany, faced her, a swivel chair in front of the kneehole. At right angles to it stood another armchair. There were papers and photographs spread out across the surface of the desk. Lying on the top was a shiny, opened-out copy of the current jewellery catalogue, attractively photographed in rich colour. From where she stood, she saw that most of the items displayed were described as Edwardian or Victorian, with a fair amount of Art Nouveau in precious and semi-precious stones, and one or two Georgian diamond pieces.

'Get a load of those prices!' Carmody said, his height giving him the advantage of being able to peer over her shoulder.

Abigail looked. Nothing much under a thousand and almost nothing under two. A lot of them rising to five figures. 'Not a place to bring Mrs C. for her Christmas present,' she said, 'though I don't suppose they're out of the way for what they are.'

'A long way out on my pay.'

'And mine. Nice, though.'

Like the rest of the place, which had a sense of quiet luxury. No feeling of rush or hurry. A good place to come – if you weren't short of a bob or two – for that special piece of jewellery to mark a particular birthday, or anniversary. To choose an engagement ring maybe, or splash out on one of the small antiques, or a piece of the fine silver displayed in the wall cabinets. Later, she promised herself time to study the collection of jewellery in the glass-topped counters. Victorian jewellery had always appealed to her.

'As soon as this lot are finished, we'll get the old man to see if there's anything missing,' she said to Carmody. 'And I'd like a special lookout kept for anything in the way of a fancy dagger, a stiletto, or some such.' Half a dozen men had already been set to comb the area around the Rose for anything which might have served as a weapon, but she didn't give much for their chances – nor even the possibility of it being found here, but they had to try.

'The nephew would know more about the stock. He works here, and the old man's more or less retired.'

'Right, we'll talk to him, then, as well. What d'you make of this, Ted?' she asked, jerking a thumb towards a foolscap pad, half covered with scribbled and indecipherable doodles, which sat next to the catalogue. It bore a large ink stain, although the gold fountain pen which lay to the side of the pad was capped. Gingerly, she reached over and lifted the corner of the pad by means of her nailfile; the ink had seeped right through to the cardboard backing and appeared to be still slightly damp. 'It must have lain on the pad for some time.'

'He was surprised while he was using it and dropped it?'

'*Was* he surprised? No forced entry, as you say, no panic button pressed. T-L thinks he was sitting down when he was stabbed. He either opened the door to his killer, or the killer had keys – in which case, he must've known who it was.'

Carmody had backed away and was looking around the shop. 'If it did happen here, whoever did it made a pretty thorough job of cleaning up afterwards. Takes some nerve, that.'

'The bleeding was mostly internal but there must have been a fair amount of gore around,' Abigail agreed. 'OK, we'll leave that until we've more to go on. Meanwhile, let's go and see what we can gather, see what he'd been doing with his day and if anything in it could have led up to this.'

11

In normal circumstances, George Fontenoy was a spruce, tall, urbanely cheerful old man. This morning he was none of these things. He seemed shrunken and bent, and looked as if he hadn't slept. He'd shaved badly, his hands trembled and there was a stain on his white shirt-front as though he had slopped his coffee. It upset him to let other people see him looking like this.

Jenny Platt fetched him from the kitchen where he'd been sitting with Matthew, making a pretence of eating some breakfast, then left him with Abigail in the sitting room and returned to the kitchen to sit with the boy.

Abigail was wandering around the big, high-ceilinged room when George came in, studying the well-polished antique furniture, the slightly shabby, oriental carpets and walls hung with pictures in heavy gilt frames. There was a fine collection of purple Stourbridge glass in the corner cabinet. A glint of old silver here and there, deeply comfortable chairs. The two men had not been without their little luxuries.

Mayo, it seemed, had not questioned George on his flying visit. He must have merely taken a quick look around – to get the feel of the scene, she presumed – leaving the interviewing to her. She took George through the necessary procedures as gently as she could, mindful of the fact that it was Fontenoy's only son who had been brutally murdered. He shook his head as if to clear it, rubbed his eyes.

'Damn sleeping pills, put me out like a light,' he grumbled. 'Iniquitous things, but I haven't been well lately and the quack insists. Takes me an hour to pull myself together in the mornings, too. Otherwise I'd have heard him go out, I'd have known.'

It was possible, of course, that something had caused Nigel Fontenoy to take it into his head to leave the house some time during the late evening. Something urgent enough to brave the foulest weather for half a century. The fact that he hadn't been wearing a coat suggested that he could have gone out in a car. Then perhaps there had been a quarrel, he'd been stabbed where he sat and then dragged from the car and dumped in the alley. Not impossible, but difficult to pull a knife and stick it into your passenger while sitting in the driving seat of your car. Especially if you were right-handed, and the attack had come from the left. He might, of course, have been driving his own car, with the attacker as passenger. The car was in the garage but could have been returned after the murder; they would have to wait for forensic examination to reveal anything there was to be revealed.

George was walking the room with tremulous steps but soon had to sit down again. He felt restless and uneasy, unable either to relax or keep moving. Still less able to calm the erratic pounding of his heart, though he knew it was bad for him to get over-excited. Concentrating on answering the young woman's questions, however, made him feel slightly better. He'd never spoken to a woman police officer before. They said she was a senior officer. A mere babe in arms, he thought her, but even thirty-five was considered over the hill these days. The damn country was being run by a kindergarten.

'Had your son quarrelled with anyone recently? Or been in a situation which had upset him? Did you have the impression anything was worrying him?'

George hesitated. 'Not more than usual. Nigel was often in a stew about something or other. Lived on his nerves, though he didn't let it show. He was inclined to be secretive about his feelings, never gave much away.' Suddenly, his eyes filled. He turned away, blew his nose loudly.

Abigail gave him time to recover before saying gently, 'You say you last saw him about half past nine, just before you went to bed. Did he give any indication he was going out later on?'

'Good God, no!' His voice still shook a little, but grew stronger as he went on. 'Why would he go out on a night like that? Especially when he was so busy? He was putting the finishing touches to the new catalogue and he intended staying up until he finished it . . . Nothing unusual in that, he never went to bed until one o'clock at least.'

'Someone may have rung him after you left him . . . arranged to meet him, perhaps? Did you hear the telephone?'

'Wouldn't hear the last trump after I've taken one of those pills! Not usually, anyway. But I did wake for a short time last night, around midnight. It was the cedar falling,' he said, already accepting as fact what his mind had told him had to be the truth. 'I dropped off again, though, eventually.'

'Was everything as you would expect to find it this morning? Everything locked up as usual – and the alarms on?'

George briefly closed his eyes. All these questions! And none of them would bring Nigel back. 'I don't know. Nigel always opened up in the mornings, but when Matthew arrived this morning, he had to use his key to get in. He has his own set of keys. I expect you'd like to speak to him?' He rose and went to the door with an alacrity born of relief and called: 'Matthew!'

Matthew was sitting at the kitchen table with Jenny Platt, who had made them both some coffee and had been taking a detailed statement from him. He knew it had to be done, and she was being prosaic and matter-of-fact about it, which helped, but Jesus, he wished she'd leave him alone to think out what he really ought to say! The elation of the previous night had left him and he felt terrible, queasy and as if his brain was stuffed with cotton wool. Just when he needed all his wits. He'd have to watch it, watch every word he said, he didn't want to start them off on the wrong tack . . . Oh God, he thought, what a mess, and prayed he wouldn't cry.

'And I suppose you'll be wanting to know where I was last night, as well,' he said savagely, turning his misery on Jenny. 'Well, if you must know, I was busy getting drunk with my mate, Joss Graham!' *So smashed out of my mind I hardly knew what I was doing, except that it was something I'd thought about for weeks and it seemed like a good idea at the time.* 'And I have the bloody hangover to prove it.'

'Dear oh dear,' Jenny said, 'no wonder you look like hell. Have some more coffee.'

Matthew glared at her then jumped up, released, when he heard George calling him, stuck his hands in his pockets and stalked into the sitting room to face yet more questions.

'My nephew – great-nephew to be precise – Matthew Wilding.' George's hand rested briefly on the boy's shoulder. 'Only just left school and joined us in the business. Joined Nigel, that is. I've been useless since my stroke so I'm more or less retired.'

'Hey, Uncle George, what are you talking about, useless?' the boy protested, but mechanically, as if he wasn't really thinking about it.

George smiled slightly. 'Plain words, Matthew. Never do any harm.' He added, with old-fashioned gravity, 'This young lady is the police officer in charge of – of all this business. She'd like to ask you some questions.'

Abigail guessed Matthew Wilding to be about eighteen, good-looking in an athletic, muscular way, with crisp dark hair, a strong nose and brown eyes in a tanned face, at the moment looking decidedly sallow. And whereas the old man, George, appeared to be making some attempt to get himself together, it was the boy who was the distraught one. He looked wretched.

'I know you've already answered a lot of questions, Matthew, but there are just a few more. First things first. You'll realize we have to consider robbery as a motive. You'll be able to go through the stock and tell us if there's anything missing?'

'Nothing obvious has been taken, I've already looked. But until we go through the stocklists, it's impossible to say for sure.'

Oh, marvellous, Abigail thought – tramping all over the scene! And wondered what Dexter would have to say to that. 'You opened up this morning – which door?'

'The side one, you can only open the front from inside.'

There were metal grilles over the double-security door and the small front window – the shop had at one time been part of the house, and you didn't need a large window to display jewellery – and the side door, according to Matthew, was locked and then bolted from inside.

'How did you get in then?'

'The bolts weren't on. It was just on the lock.'

'Nigel wouldn't have left it unbolted,' George said sharply, then fell abruptly silent, realizing, as everyone else did, that the door had been left unbolted because Nigel had made his last exit that way, voluntarily or not. Further questions produced the information that the only other way into the shop was through the house itself and, like the side door, these doors were always bolted on the inside.

Matthew said suddenly to George, half defiant, 'I've rung Christine to let her know what's happened, Uncle George. She was out when I first rang, but she's coming down straightaway now. Have I done right?'

His attitude was wary, as if he was expecting a rebuff, but an expression of intense relief crossed Fontenoy's face. 'Good lad. Quite right. Ought to have thought of it m'self. Christine will know what to do.'

'Who is Christine?' Abigail asked.

'My stepmother. She used to work here – well, more than *work* . . . There's nothing she doesn't know about the business. She only left when she married my father.'

'Thank God, here she is now,' George said, as voices were heard downstairs and light footsteps could be heard ascending. 'She must have dropped everything and come immediately.'

'Well, Christine would, wouldn't she?' Matthew said.

He flung himself down into the chair, his hands driven deep into his pockets, as an attractive, red-headed woman entered the room like a brisk breeze. Her hair, lighter and brighter than Abigail's by several shades, lit the room like a lamp in a dark corner. She had eyes of a vivid blue-green, a gorgeous figure, a generous mouth that was a trifle too wide for beauty, and seemed to charge the room with her energy. The overhanging pall of misery seemed to lift a little.

'Oh, George!' she said. George stood up and put his arms around her. For a moment she laid her head against his shoulder, throwing out a hand to Matthew, which, after a moment, he grasped hard, then dropped, embarrassed. After this, she seemed to give herself a little shake and asked to be told exactly what had happened, paying careful attention to what was said. 'Has the stock been checked yet? Right, I'll give Matthew a hand to go through it,' she announced.

'Oh, all right,' Matthew replied, without much visible enthusiasm.

'Come on, Matt, buck up, you won't feel so bad if you've something to do,' she chivvied him, her tone suggesting that she herself would not be averse to having something practical to occupy herself with.

'I'm afraid we shall have to ask you to wait until our Forensic team's finished,' Abigail told her.

The other woman looked momentarily disconcerted but then nodded. Nothing much, Abigail guessed, would throw her for long. She was dressed with perfect coordination and if she'd dropped everything to come over here then full marks for efficiency. Her cream sweater and tan slacks were complemented by a chestnut suede jacket, soft leather boots, big gold earrings and a chunky matching necklace. Her hair swung like a bell. An expensive bell, thought Abigail, who knew what her own cropping had cost.

It was only when she saw the expression in those extraordinary turquoise eyes that she knew that Christine Wilding, too, was filled with misery and despair, and wondered why.

The SOCO team worked on, continuing their examination, fingerprinting the glass cases, doors and door jambs, sticky-taping for fibres, vacuum-cleaning every inch of the carpeted floor. They took away the foolscap pad with the ink stain on it, and cut out a large square of carpet. DC Napier took photographs from every possible angle. Sergeant Dexter estimated they would finish in the shop within a day and would begin on the rest of the premises the following day. Christine Wilding packed a bag for old George and bore him off to Ham Lane.

The following day, Matthew and Christine Wilding were able to check through the stock. Matthew rang to say when they had finished, and Abigail went along to the shop to get the details, taking Carmody with her.

It appeared that two things were missing: a gold and lapis-lazuli seal ring (though it was possible that this might have been taken out of stock and worn by Nigel himself, something he was in the habit of doing). The other was a gold chain and pendant, set with amethysts and a diamond, worth something under fifteen hundred pounds.

'Though why that, and nothing else, I find it hard to understand,' Christine Wilding frowned. 'Compared with all this other stuff it was nothing in terms of value. And besides, it needed cleaning and the clasp replacing. That's why it wasn't on display.'

'Nothing special about it, then?' asked Carmody.

It was Matthew who answered. 'Not really. It was part of a private collection that came in a few weeks ago, belonging to some old woman who'd died, but nothing of it was worth anything to speak of. Nothing worth murdering anybody for.'

Carmody, who'd known people mugged and killed for the price of a packet of fags or the next fix, didn't disillusion him. He asked if it was possible that Nigel Fontenoy himself had sent the pendant for repairs to the broken clasp and forgotten to record the fact. A quick telephone call to the repairers, however, confirmed that they knew nothing about it.

'Nothing else missing?'

Matthew shook his head, then Christine gave a sudden exclamation. She'd remembered a wrapped parcel, kept at the back of the safe, its contents apparently unknown to anyone but Nigel.

'Mr Fontenoy,' Abigail turned to George. 'Have you any idea what might have been in it?'

'What? Oh, certainly not. Not at all. It was Nigel's personal property and he never said what was in it.'

'Matthew?'

'I remember the parcel, it was a nuisance, always in the way – but I never saw it opened.'

'Oh, well, he must have got rid of it, and whatever was in it.' Christine described the parcel. 'It was a box of some kind, I think, wood or metal by the feel of it. Not cardboard, I would've thought.'

'How big?'

She sketched shoebox dimensions in the air.

'And you've no idea what was inside it?'

'Papers, I suspect. Nigel used to refer to it as his retirement pension.'

'Insurances, share certificates, things like that?'

'I suppose so, but they wouldn't be much use to anyone else, would they?'

Matthew said suddenly, 'He took a parcel with him when he went to London, yesterday. It could've been the same box – it was that sort of shape and size. But he didn't get back here until after we'd closed and I'd gone home, so I don't know if he brought it back.'

'Rewind it and let's all have another listen,' Abigail said several hours later, back at Milford Road Police Station.

While Carmody fiddled about and then pressed the play-back switch of Nigel Fontenoy's answering machine, now standing on a desk in the CID room, away from the frenzied activity of an incident room in the first stages of a murder inquiry, Abigail perched on the corner, skimming through her notes as she waited.

The last few days of Nigel Fontenoy's life had, it appeared, followed their normal pattern, except for the visit to London on the day he died. There, his appointment diary revealed, he'd had an appointment with a Mr Alec Macaudle, of Jermyn's, the big London-based jewellery conglomerate; further searches had brought to light a lengthy correspondence between the two men, the subject of which was the imminent takeover of Fontenoy's by Jermyn's, something

90

George Fontenoy insisted he knew nothing about. In a file marked 'Personal' they also found a copy of a letter to Jake Wilding, Matthew's father, the contents of which were judged promising enough to warrant following up.

Meanwhile, there was Nigel's answering machine to consider, which Carmody now fast-forwarded, bypassing the other messages, deemed to be of no interest at the moment, until he came to the one they wanted to hear again – a curt, unidentified message which merely said, *OK. see you. Same place, same time.*

There was a tantalizing quality about the voice, as if it ought to be recognizable. But it showed some distortion, whether deliberate or not, and, since neither George Fontenoy, Christine nor Matthew Wilding had been able (or willing) to identify it, it was hardly surprising that none of the investigating team could either, even after listening to it several times.

Carmody finally gave up and switched it off.

Abigail said, 'Get me Jermyn's on the line. I'd better speak to this Mr Macaudle.'

But he had, it seemed, left that morning for Switzerland and would be away for the next few days. If Mr Fontenoy had left anything in the way of a parcel with Mr Macaudle, a starchy female voice informed her, he would not have failed to mention it, but she would take a look to make sure. It was a foregone conclusion, before she rang back, that her answer would be negative. Yes, she would leave a message for Mr Macaudle to ring Inspector Moon when he returned.

12

Gil Mayo always hoped the day might come when he had all his cases neatly stitched up before a new one materialized, but since his was not a particularly optimistic nature he had to concede that this was pie in the sky. Meanwhile, out of necessity, he'd become an expert at running several complex cases together – such as preparing airtight evidence for a prosecution on the one hand, while familiarizing himself with the details of a new investigation on the other, at the same time as keeping the facts of something else in his head. The last week had been like that, hellish, but things had improved, and today offered a bonus: the court hearing had been adjourned, leaving him free to concentrate on the Fontenoy murder with Abigail Moon.

He would have preferred to be working with Kite, but this was impossible, and there were compensations. She was prettier than Kite, for one thing, and smelled nicer. She was wearing a sharp, fresh scent, a greenish-brown suit that matched her eyes, and her bronze wavy hair shone with life and vitality. All of which he'd had plenty chance to appreciate as she drove him up to Ham Lane to talk to Jake Wilding.

The venue was at Wilding's suggestion; it was mid-morning, but evidently he'd decided that business wasn't pressing enough to preclude taking time off. Or perhaps he could work from home.

An air of suppressed excitement hung around him. Was he, Mayo wondered, one of those men who were turned on by the idea of violence? His demeanour didn't suggest deep sorrow at the news of Nigel Fontenoy's death, yet when he was asked about his connections with the dead man, his reply was unsteady.

'My God, I can't believe it! We'd always been close, old Nigel and me. We were cousins, went to school together, my son worked for him – but of course, you know that, you've spoken to Matthew.'

And would need to speak to him again. However, it wasn't Matthew Wilding who was concerning Mayo at the moment, but his father. And money. There was money involved in all this . . . shown by the copy letter found in Nigel Fontenoy's files, indicating that Jake Wilding was in debt for an undisclosed sum to his cousin.

Why had Wilding needed to borrow from Fontenoy? The jeweller had been comfortably off by most standards, even allowing for the fact that the jewellery trade was, understandably, one of the first to suffer in a recession, but as far as real money went, he couldn't have been in the same league as Wilding. Ah well, Carmody had said, Jake Wilding was a clever-dick builder and property developer, and everyone knew what that meant. Slippery as a bucketful of eels, not averse to turning a quick penny by cutting a few corners, adept at manipulating planning regulations, used to getting away with murder. An unscrupulous sod, with half the town council probably in his pocket. Carmody was Liverpool Irish and said he spoke from experience.

'Nice to hear strictly unbiased opinions!' Mayo commented drily. 'I shall want something better than that.'

But certainly risk and living on a financial knife-edge was the name of the game to men of Jake Wilding's sort, and even a small loan might be important to him. Inquiries had been made about him. He had reputedly started with nothing. His mother had been a Fontenoy, old George Fontenoy's sister, but any money she had brought to the marriage had soon been squandered by her husband, Jake's father, also a builder, and eventually a bankrupt. Later, by Jake's own efforts, the firm had risen, phoenix-like, from the ashes; he had by now built himself a little empire. Private sector housing was still his main business but he was said also to have a stake in a local taxi-cab and bus firm, to dabble in broadcasting and television franchises and to have a half share in the local football club. He had interests in road construction and was much in evidence where local authority building schemes were concerned.

His lifestyle was impressive. Ham Lane was a pleasant, quiet lane of substantially built, luxurious houses, all of them with large, secluded gardens backing on to a wood. Abigail and Mayo had caught a glimpse of a swimming pool through the windows of the old conservatory when they arrived, and there was a tennis court. They'd exchanged glances, eyebrows raised.

The house was large and its interior was flooded with light and furnished with an expensive and clever mixture of modern furniture and antiques. The soft furnishings in richly patterned jewel colours glowed against walls the colour of clotted cream. As well as some very beautiful pictures, there were several striking modern bronze sculptures: on a small table near Abigail was a polished female nude kneeling on a sea shore, the curl of a huge wave behind her echoing the curve of a slender back. Without having to be told, knowing nothing of fine art, she looked at it and knew it was outstanding. Somebody here had style and taste.

It may have been Christine Wilding. She was something of a work of art herself, dressed today in a soft angora sweater the colour of apricots, immaculately made up, heavy topaz jewellery in an antique setting round her throat. She had supplied tea and now sat back in her chair, her shapely legs crossed, listening without comment, watching her husband as he stated that the last time he had seen Nigel Fontenoy had been at ten o'clock the previous evening.

The appointment hadn't been recorded in Nigel's meticulously kept diary, though Wilding wouldn't necessarily have known that, and Mayo said sharply, 'Did you make the appointment by telephone, or through a message on his answerphone?'

'Neither. I made a personal call at the shop earlier in the week. I don't remember what day but Matthew was there and he can probably tell you.'

'Can anybody verify this meeting last night? Did anybody

see you there – Mr George Fontenoy, maybe?' Mayo asked.

'No, he'd gone to bed. He's an old man and he hasn't been well. Nigel was expecting me and let me in through the side door, so unless anybody was passing and happened to see me going in, I'm afraid there's nothing to confirm that I actually was there.'

'Wasn't it rather late for a business appointment?'

'I had a previous engagement and couldn't make it earlier. Nigel didn't mind. He said he'd be working in the shop, anyway.'

'What was the meeting about?'

Wilding shrugged. 'Nothing of any importance.'

Mayo wasn't letting him get away with that. 'Oh? Discussing the repayment of that loan he'd made to you wasn't important?'

'Loan?' That had touched a nerve. His eyes flickered. They were brown, quick dark brown, and he had rough, fairish hair that he constantly ran his fingers through. A full-lipped, sensuous mouth, a craggy face. Late forties. His body was younger than his face, and disciplined, moving like an actor's, with casual grace. There was a strong family likeness to his uncle, old George Fontenoy – strange, Abigail thought, when Fontenoy's son had borne little resemblance to his father. Funny things, genes, popping up where you least expected them.

Recovering quickly from his surprise, he smiled crookedly and said, 'It hasn't taken you long to find that out! Well, you've obviously seen a copy of the letter he sent me, so there's no point in denying it.'

Nigel Fontenoy had been a precise kind of man, where business was concerned. His papers were in apple pie order. Copies were kept. His appointment book had been clearly written up. It made their job easier.

Mayo said, 'I've seen the letter and I have to say that the tone of it didn't suggest the sort of amicable relationship you say you had with him, Mr Wilding. If anyone asked me, I'd have said the tone was peremptory.'

'Oh, that was just Nigel covering his back ... for the record,' he said, evidently thinking fast, and perhaps

95

improvising as he went along. 'In case I reneged. The point was, until recently he'd been quite willing to let it ride until I was in a better position to repay, but then he'd found himself temporarily in difficulties and he wanted it back. Anyway, it was all sorted last night. He agreed to leave things as they were, though as it turns out, it wouldn't have been necessary.' The underlying elation Mayo had sensed when they first met was back again.

'There's been an improvement in your financial position?'

'Let's say in certain prospects,' Wilding returned with a smile that hinted at secret satisfaction. On the other side of the hearth, Christine Wilding reached forward and poured herself another cup of tea.

'Would that be because Mr Fontenoy has left his share of the business and half of what else he has to your son?' The other half, according to George Fontenoy, was to go to his sister's three children in New Zealand.

Wilding didn't like that, didn't like them knowing, and possibly not the implications either. His smile became rather more fixed, and a different element entered his manner, not so easily placeable. 'I don't see what that has to do with my situation. It's Matthew he's left it to, not me,' he said shortly.

'But it's still in the family. Might he not want to invest in your business?' Abigail suggested.

'Matthew?' He laughed shortly. 'Not likely!'

'Jake,' said Christine, quietly.

'All right, forget I said that. It's only that I'm not sure that leaving all that money to Matthew – to anybody that age, for that matter – was a wise move on Nigel's part. Matthew's barely nineteen and he hasn't yet made his mind up what he wants to do with his life – but I'm willing to bet it won't be running Cedar House Antiques for the rest of it, if that's what Nigel was hoping! More likely throwing it away on rally cars.'

Mayo well knew that these were the sort of disparaging remarks fathers might be expected to make about troublesome teenage sons – though perhaps with less bitterness. Wilding and his son evidently didn't get on, or at any rate, didn't see eye to eye. But then, both of them might be difficult to live with, in their different ways. Looking steadily at Wilding, he said, 'You do realize that you were the last person to have seen Mr Fontenoy alive?'

He was picked up sharply. '*Known* to have seen him, yes. But someone else must have seen him after I did, because I can tell you he was still very much alive when I left him. I didn't kill him. He could be an irritating bastard, but most of us can be at one time or another, I suppose.'

'Irritating? In what way, irritating?'

'That's neither here nor there,' Wilding answered shortly, possibly with a belated realization that the remark might have been better left unsaid.

'So you parted on good terms?'

'I've already said as much, yes.'

'How long did you stay with him?'

'Just under an hour, I should think. Anyway, it was some time after eleven when I got back home. I'm not sure of the exact time.'

'Quarter past, actually,' said Christine.

Jake waited until the sound of the car engine had died away. His eyes stayed fixed on Christine, with an expression she found baffling. She sat waiting for him to bring the subject up and eventually he did.

'Why did you lie to them?' he asked. 'About the time I got home?'

Christine drew in her breath. Why did he *think*, for God's sake? To protect him, of course! And – well, yes, maybe herself, too. She had a lot to lose. She answered stiffly, obliquely, 'Why did you bring me those flowers today?' *And wine, and delicious pâté. Almost as if in celebration, rather than mourning a death. As a bribe?*

'To cheer you up. I knew how upset you'd be about Nigel. You always did have a soft spot for him, didn't you?'

Upset? What a word to use! What a singularly inept choice of word to describe her feelings. She felt her temper rising. 'Yes, I'm *upset*, but not because of what you think. I'm upset because he's dead, because the way he died is horrible.' *And because I can't – I simply cannot – bear the thought that you might have been responsible. Any more than I can bear the thought of the suspicions going through your mind.* But her anger evaporated as suddenly as it had threatened. She said, on a dying fall, 'There was never anything between us, Jake – except a promise, which he broke.'

'What sort of promise?'

Her answer was a while in coming, she was wondering how to phrase what she had to say in a way that would be acceptable to him. 'You know he was thinking of selling out?' she said, at last.

'Selling out?' Jake's eyes snapped. No, he hadn't known that, and was put out that he hadn't been told. He always felt he had a right to know everything that was going on, to have his finger on every pulse, although Nigel's affairs could really have had very little importance for him, personally.

'Well, he was. To Jermyn's – the big London jewellers. He's been negotiating with them for over a year. And all the time, he was promising that he'd make me a partner . . .' Jake looked thunderstruck and the injustice of Nigel's behaviour struck her anew. She said bitterly, 'He wasn't ever much of a businessman, I've no need to tell you that. I could always manage things so much better and he knew it – and was glad of it. Until he had a better offer. But he still went on promising, when he knew, all the time.'

Jake was rendered silent by all this. At last he said, 'So you married me, instead?'

'I married you, yes, but not instead of anything! Jake, why are we quarrelling? Aren't things bad enough?'

Jake had wanted Christine from the first moment he saw her, admiring not only her beautifully shaped body, her vibrant hair, those amazing eyes, but her smartness and the competence with which she managed Nigel's business, the way she tried to make life more comfortable for everyone. He'd laid siege to her and wasn't surprised when she accepted the glamorous invitations he was able to offer. Most women did. But then he'd gradually become aware of a continuing need for her, a desire for a longer-term relationship other than mere physical satisfaction. The fact that he'd come to love her hit him like a thunderbolt and had made him, hitherto so certain of himself, unsure. He'd scarcely been able to believe it when she agreed to be his wife.

'Christine, Christine!' He took a step forwards and put his arms round her.

She leaned against his strength, knowing without question now that she loved him and would be prepared to do more than merely lie for him. But she still didn't know where he'd been until nearly one o'clock that morning.

Back in the incident room, surrounded by members of the team, the air thick with cigarette smoke, incessantly ringing telephones and the clack of printers, Abigail said, 'For what it's worth, his wife swears he was back by quarter past eleven. But I wouldn't like to bet on how much it *is* worth. I think she's covering for him, although if he arrived at the shop at ten, as he said, there'd be time to do all he had to do, dump the body and get back home by that time. It's not all that far from Nailers' Yard to Ham Lane, especially by car.'

'And who's to say he didn't arrive for his appointment before ten?' a DC asked.

'Unlikely, if he intended killing Nigel. It would've been too risky. He couldn't be sure that the old man would've been in bed by then. And there'd still be people about – he couldn't have planned on the storm keeping everyone indoors.'

'True,' Carmody put in. 'And would he have made an appointment at all if he'd intended murder? Run the risk of having Nigel write it down in his diary, knowing how finicky he was about that sort of thing? I'll bet it was only by chance he hadn't noted it down, anyway, maybe because he was busy in the shop when Wilding called.'

'I want to play that tape again before we send it over to the experts to see what they can do with it. See if we can make out a bit more.'

'Let's have a bit of hush, then,' Carmody said to the room at large, slotting the tape into the machine.

'You can buy a fun gizmo now that deliberately distorts your voice,' Farrar offered while the tape was being fast-forwarded through the Mickey Mouse squawks of the other calls on the machine, business calls which had by now been followed up, vetted, then eliminated.

'You can also put a handkerchief over the mouthpiece, or hold your nose,' added Jenny Platt drily.

'Listen, can't you?' Carmody released the button.

OK. See you. Same place, same time.

Not nearly enough to go on.

'But there *is* something maddeningly familiar about it,' Abigail said, nibbling her finger.

They grouped around it, listening to the recording several times but nobody could make any constructive suggestion as to the owner of the voice. Just as the next replay began, in walked DC Deeley.

'It's Tom Callaghan,' he said.

Deeley was looked upon as the station beefcake, the good-humoured butt of CID ragging. Put down as a bit thick, but known for stumbling on things. Dead lucky, they said, uncharitably, not giving him the credit for the sharpness that was (admittedly well-hidden) beneath the surface, not liking it that he had an uncanny knack of being right.

He was in this case. 'That's it — it does sound like Callaghan!' Abigail agreed, after a moment. 'Well done, Pete!'

'Tom Callaghan? *The* Tom Callaghan?' asked Carmody.

'It *is* him!' said Jenny, a regular viewer of his programme, though not by any means because she was a fan of his. It was always as well to know the opposition, in her opinion.

'There's hope for you yet, Pete,' said Farrar, annoyed that he hadn't identified the voice himself.

13

Hands in pockets, Ted Carmody stood gazing at concrete mixers, squared-off piles of bricks and breeze-blocks covered in polythene, plus all the other untidy paraphernalia on the Wilding building site, the as yet unmade up road cutting a red, sandy swathe through the middle. Dusk was falling and work had stopped for the day.

Building had started at the top of the site and was working downhill. Only about half a dozen houses were as yet occupied, their curtains already drawn against the dark, houses and families drawn in tight to themselves. It wasn't a comfortable place to live, not yet.

'Like I said, you'll have to come across yonder to see what I mean,' said the man Carmody was talking to, a small, wiry type with a bald head and a luxuriant moustache that tried hard to compensate. He was wearing jeans and a quilted anorak and his face was tight with suppressed anger.

The site was otherwise deserted. Carmody had timed himself to arrive after the workmen had knocked off but before it was too dark to see properly, wanting to do some poking around. He'd often found it paid dividends. Like now, though in this case it was ma'am who'd suggested it.

Fontenoy's car, after being thoroughly examined by Forensics, had been passed as clean. Likewise Jake Wilding's, which had also, under protest, been impounded for forensic examination.

'But he's still the best we've got – and if he did it, he must've had access to some form of transport. Get somebody to take a look at what's on his building site, Ted,' Abigail had said. Carmody had chosen to come himself.

He didn't think much of the site security. A locked

compound with a high wire fence enclosed raw materials, but any competent burglar could have made mincemeat out of the lock in five minutes. As well as a big JCB there were sundry trucks, bulldozers and a lot of other machinery hanging around. Nice class of house, though. Upmarket prices and more spacious than you'd think, albeit the gardens were on the cramped side. Carmody reckoned himself a good judge of a house, he'd moved around enough in his time. They preferred older houses, he and Maureen, with a sizeable garden, a solid, between-the-wars job, built when labour costs were lower and land not at such a premium.

He'd done his poking around and not come up with anything until, as he emerged from one of the almost completed houses, this man, who gave his name as Dave Hodgson, had appeared out of the growing dusk.

'You're the police,' he stated.

'Sergeant Carmody,' Carmody said, seeing no reason not to admit it, no longer surprised that people recognized his calling at a glance, though he couldn't see how they did it. His feet were no bigger and no flatter than the next man's, he practically never went around saying 'Ullo, ullo, what 'ave we 'ere, then?' But people knew, invariably.

'It's the look, love,' Maureen said comfortably. 'You've got that way of looking at folks.'

He knew what she meant: he recognized it in his mates, that searching, non-committal look they all developed through the need to know, and the effort not to judge. Cynical, some thought it.

He looked now at Hodgson, who said he was a garage mechanic himself, but that was by the way, he was here as a member of the local conservation society. 'And we're not just a load of old Nimbys, neither. Some of us have real principles,' he stated belligerently, and repeated that there was something the sergeant ought to know about, that would interest him very much.

Carmody decided to humour him and followed him across the site and through a smashed stretch of fencing to a large piece of land whereon, enclosed within a flattened barbed wire fence and surrounded by fields of meadowgrass, stood the remains of what had once been Forde Manor, now nothing more than rubble. A fourteenth-century listed building, according to the *Advertiser*, reporting its spectacular collapse, an unlucky casualty of the storm which had arisen on the night Nigel Fontenoy had died. Pictures of the house in its prime had appeared in a central spread devoted to 'Lavenstock's Night of Mayhem'. Many-gabled, timber-framed, with twisted chimneys and roofs sweeping to the ground, lattice windows peering from under the eaves, the house was said to have had a solar and a priest's hole, a spere-truss – whatever that might be – in the hall, and God knows what else. It had been a unique and irreplaceable example of medieval cruck construction. But derelict and dangerous for years, its floors and ceilings collapsed, its walls cracked, its foundations shaky. Like the Cedar House tree, it might have been struck by lightning, or the wind might have simply shaken it to bits. Whatever had caused it, it had gone down, collapsed into a mighty heap of rubble – hammer-beam roof, linenfold panelling, dog-leg staircases and all.

'It could've been restored, made into a showplace. Now it's just a bit more of our national heritage gone,' Hodgson mourned bitterly.

A pity, Carmody agreed. You didn't like to see part of the past disappear. On the other hand, maybe it had outlived its usefulness. Everything comes to an end. 'Act of God?' he suggested, though having guessed by now what was coming.

'God acted bloody conveniently for somebody, then! For the person who wanted it down to build a hypermarket. D'you know who owns this site? Jake Wilding, that's who! As well as that across the road. Must be laughing like a bloody drain.' Hodgson balled his fists into his pockets as if otherwise he might punch the first thing handy. 'Look at that!' he said, withdrawing his hand and pointing.

Carmody studied what the press photograph, taken from the front, hadn't shown: two sets of wide tyre-tracks, deeply bitten into the mud, leading to the rear of the house, and back to the building site.

'Are you making a complaint, sir?'

'Not yet, but we shall be. Our society's meeting tonight to

decide tactics. But I'll tell you something: this house has weathered storms as bad as that for nigh on six hundred years. It was shored up, there was no reason why it should've collapsed – not unless the props were knocked away, deliberate. That way, it'd have gone down like a house of cards. There was a preservation order on it but that's no protection against a man with a JCB.'

'It'd be a daft thing to try. Dangerous, on a night like that.'

'Depends how much you want to build a multi-million pound hypermarket, doesn't it?'

Funny how often the very word 'hypermarket' was enough to send some people's blood pressure up to danger level. 'Would one be a bad thing, out here? What about service to the community – to the folks that live over there?' Carmody ventured, indicating the extensive spread of small, new houses which lay behind them, forming the Ashmount Estate, built right on the edge of the green belt. 'It's a long way out of town. Not many shops, I should think.'

Hodgson said, 'That's where I live. And I can tell you, this community needs another hypermarket like we need a hole in the head. What's another mile or so to pick up the shopping? We've all got cars. What we soon won't have is peace and quietness, a bit of real country, somewhere safe for the kids to play, if places like this are gradually being eaten into.'

There wasn't much to be done about it, though, Carmody felt, now that it was a *fait accompli*. 'I take your point. But they can't make him put it together again.'

'Can't they just? I wouldn't be too sure. There have been precedents.' After a moment's thought, however, Hodgson was forced to agree. 'You're bloody right, not a feasible proposition, is it? Not a job like this, something of this age and condition. A fine that he'll pay out of his petty cash is probably about all they can do. One thing you can be sure of, though. He won't damn well profit by it! Not if I and the members of my society have anything to do with it.'

Carmody left him, staring gloomily at the ruin, brooding.

He was on his way home, but before starting out, he used his car radio to ring in to the station and speak to DI Moon, asking for permission to have vehicles on the building site checked by Forensics. 'Think we might've struck gold,' he said laconically. 'There's a Bedford pick-up with a wooden floor and some stains on it that look a bit suspicious. Covered with brick dust and cement and plaster until I'd brushed it away. Might be paint, or rust, but might not.'

It might, of course, be blood which had got there quite legitimately. Of its nature, the building trade was a rough one, a hard hat trade, with accidents an occupational hazard. Bricks could fall on your head, trap your toes, Carmody reasoned. Take one unwary step and you could fall off a scaffold, he had no doubt. Cuts and abrasions, skinning your hands, must be a regular occurrence, of as little concern as a flea bite.

'All the same,' Abigail said, 'we want it checked. And the Accident Report book as well, to be going on with.' She listened carefully to what he had to say about the house. 'Any indications what time it was knocked down – if it was?'

'Not much doubt about that. This guy Hodgson claims that he and one or two other people heard what they thought was an almighty clap of thunder about half past one, quarter to two.'

'Are you thinking what I'm thinking, Ted?'

'If you're thinking Jake Wilding could've been lying about times and did it himself after topping Nigel, then yeah, I am.'

'Unlikely. Wouldn't the house have been the last thing on his mind?'

'Well, if it was knocked down deliberate like, to make it look like an accident, it must've been the storm that gave somebody the idea. And if Wilding was hyped-up after doing the murder, well –'

Yes, Wilding's judgement might well not have been as cool and clear as it ought to have been – and if that much money was at stake, maybe he'd thought it was a risk worth taking.

It was a complication they didn't need, she thought as she drove home. But one way or another, it looked as though it was only a matter of time before they had Wilding sewn up.

A name slid into her mind and she thought of the interview she and Mayo had had with Callaghan earlier in the day, and suddenly she didn't feel quite so certain about Wilding.

14

The cottage where Abigail lived was barely three miles out of Lavenstock, in an unconsidered backwater that was neither suburb nor what Hodgson would have called real country, and in bad and therefore affordable condition when she'd bought it. It sat surrounded by flat fields and the uncompromising bulk of a big, bare hill to the rear, halfway down a rutted track which led to a farm round the back of the hill. It was square and solid, built of Victorian stock bricks with a slate roof, four windows at the front and a door to the middle, like a child's drawing. The garden was yet to be. It was not beautiful but Abigail loved it to death.

By the time she'd paid the deposit and forked out for the repairs necessary to make it habitable, and it had been pronounced sound in wind and limb, there hadn't been much money left, so it had been furnished by raiding her parents' attic and with bits and pieces found in second-hand shops. She'd discovered a solid, old oak dining table that she'd stripped of its tacky old varnish and which was now gradually responding to the coats of polish she gave it when she had time, and a big, shabby, comfy old sofa her mother was planning to help her recover. She'd put up some bookshelves and hoped they'd stand up to the weight of her books, bought a bed and acquired a wardrobe, and that was more or less as far as she'd got. She didn't mind waiting for the right pieces to turn up, because she hoped the cottage would be a long-term thing.

A can of soup and a warm granary roll for supper hadn't been what she'd had in mind when she first came to live here. She'd promised herself proper, civilized meals, but she'd underestimated the strength of will needed to cope with cooking after a gruelling day, not to mention remembering to shop for the raw materials. There was always something she'd forgotten, or else whatever she chose needed slicing, grating, pounding, plus four hours in the oven. In any event, cooking took second place, as did everything else, when she was working on a case. And every*one* else, too, it had to be said. All or nothing, that had always been Abigail, no half measures.

The fire had taken hold by the time she was ready to eat, and the logs crackled comfortably, the flames leaped and threw interesting shadows on the wall. She was free for what was left of the evening. No bills in the post to think about. No messages left on her answering machine. She took a tray and sat on the rug in front of the fire. After a stiff gin and tonic, the scratch meal tasted all right. But she couldn't relax and turn her thoughts off. She was wound up and the mechanism wouldn't run down.

The telephone rang. It was Ben Appleyard, the new editor of the *Advertiser*. Late thirties, a fast talker, dynamic. 'Abigail, how are you? Great evening, that dinner last week, wasn't it? Shall we do it again? And sooner rather than later, huh?'

Abigail felt herself smiling. 'I'd love it, Ben, but I'm on a case right now –'

'I know. The Fontenoy job. I'm not here to pressure you, love, but watch this space as soon as you're free.' In her head, she visualized him: very tall, thin as a whip, dark, narrow face, humorous eyes. Her toes curled up with pleasure. He asked suddenly, 'What are you having for supper tonight?'

'*Filet de saumon en croûte* with asparagus and new potatoes. *Champagne délice* to follow.'

'I knew you wouldn't be eating tinned soup,' he came back with uncanny accuracy, and a laugh in his voice. 'One of these days, I'll teach you to cook properly for yourself. Bet you haven't climbed that hill behind your house yet, either?'

'You're a bully.'

'So I am. Look, I wouldn't have disturbed you but I have

something that might interest you about Tom Callaghan.'

'And why should you think I'd be interested in Tom Callaghan?'

'You know what they say about little birds and journalists.'

'OK, Ben, what is it?'

He was immediately serious. 'About five or six years ago his daughter walked under a bus. On purpose, according to the bus driver. He swore at the inquest that he saw her step off the pavement quite deliberately. He slammed his brakes on but he was too late. Witnesses confirmed that he hadn't a chance, poor sod. She was only sixteen.'

Sixteen! God. 'Anything to suggest why she might've done it?'

'Nothing at the inquest, but afterwards there was talk about a man, a much older man. She wasn't pregnant or anything, but a whisper from one of her friends later said she was badly depressed over the affair.'

'And the man?' Abigail asked, with a sense of inevitability.

'Not a certainty you'd wager your best silk knickers on, but a name did come up. Nigel Fontenoy.'

'Fontenoy? One of Callaghan's best friends, I suppose you realize? He played golf with him right up to last Sunday.'

'Perhaps Callaghan never heard the rumour. Perhaps he's been biding his time.'

'And perhaps the rumour was malicious gossip.'

'Perhaps. But it wasn't the first time Fontenoy had been mentioned in connection with a young girl.'

'Where did you hear all this, Ben?'

'Have a word with our Nan, she'll put you in the picture.' Nan Randall was the leading feature writer on the *Advertiser*, a mine of information on everything pertaining to Lavenstock. Abigail promised she would.

'Well, that's it,' Ben said, 'that's why I rang. I'll leave you in peace now, love. Don't forget to keep your door locked to strange men. Sweet dreams.'

'Sweet dreams. And thanks, Ben.'

'Think nothing of it.'

When he'd rung off, she checked both doors, though she knew she'd locked them. There was a name for that. But she *liked* living alone, she reminded herself. She'd nearly made a big mistake in that direction once, and not so long ago, either. A mistake she didn't intend to repeat, one that wouldn't have done her career much good, though her decision to end the affair had ultimately been to the advantage of both of them. The man in question, a married man, a DC junior to her in rank, had since mended his marriage and moved away. In future, any man in her life would be well outside her professional sphere. How far outside it could Ben Appleyard be considered? Or come to be considered as the man in her life? She was comfortable with him, they shared the same sense of humour. He made no demands, and wasn't likely to. He'd never married but was demonstrably heterosexual. He too was ambitious, maybe a bit ruthless, but what of it? They looked at life in the same way, she thought, pleased with the idea, as she made sure the curtains were drawn tight.

The cottage was very isolated, her mother had said doubtfully – what about a dog, but who needed guard dogs when they had the Fossdykes and Fido at the end of the lane?

The Fossdykes lived in a white bungalow at the end of the lane, an elderly, white-haired couple, so alike they resembled a matched pair of garden gnomes. They wore track suits in primary colours and woolly hats, and kept an animal as big as themselves: huge, black, woolly-coated, with a baying bark like a bloodhound, said to be a dog, but arguably a bear.

Because of cows which grazed in the field, the gate had to be kept shut and because of the dog the ways of getting through without either Fossdyke pouncing on her with offers of help and information on settling in every time she passed were already many and devious. But her neighbours were kind, they were elderly and didn't see many people and Abigail hadn't the heart to brush them off too often, even when she'd had a long day or was about to start another.

Tonight, with Ben's warning still echoing in her ears, she was actively glad of their presence, not to mention the dog's. She poked the fire, an impulse she'd discovered to be deeply satisfying and quite irresistible, not only to herself but apparently to everyone else who visited the cottage. She curled up beside it, thinking about what Ben had said about Tom Callaghan, and the interview with him.

He hadn't been pleased. Being interrogated by the police formed no part of Callaghan's image. They'd found him working in his apartment, informally dressed in slacks and a black cotton sweater, his papers spread over the extensive matt-surfaced teak desk placed so that it overlooked the river and the hills in the far distance.

He made no bones about having left the message on the answerphone. Yes, he'd called Nigel, he said impatiently. Yes, possibly he had forgotten to leave his name, he couldn't remember whether he had or not, but Nigel was familiar enough with the sound of his voice, for God's sake, after all these years. The message had only been to confirm their more or less regular Sunday morning golf date.

Callaghan then relaxed, smiling apologetically, once more the media person. 'Sorry if I'm a bit edgy, I'm on my usual deadline for the programme. And shattered about Nigel, naturally. It's not every day you hear one of your best friends has been murdered.' Smoothing back his wavy white hair, he leaned back and crossed outstretched legs. He was shorter than he appeared on TV but tougher looking, the sweater stretched over a taut body that was evidently kept well in trim. His apartment, too, was at odds with the warm, sympathetic man projected to the public each week, its furnishings Spartan to a degree. For a man of his profession, there were surprisingly few books, no pictures and only one photograph, prominently displayed, which Abigail now realized must have been of his daughter.

'How long have you known Mr Fontenoy?' Mayo had asked.

'Since we were at school together. It was a shock when I heard he was dead, I can tell you. Makes you aware of your own mortality, though hopefully most of us will be spared *that*.'

'How did you get on with each other?'

'I've told you, we were friends.'

'That was when you were at school together. People change.'

'Indeed they do,' Callaghan answered smoothly, 'but not us. Not in that way. We kept up our friendship.' He smiled again, the famous, all-purpose smile, embracing everyone, directed at no one. The eyes that twinkled so charmingly from the small screen were, in real life, as cold as agates.

Abigail knew intuitively that he was lying. Glancing at Mayo, she'd seen that he knew it, too. To protect the nice guy image was what they'd then suspected, but however concerned he was to conceal it, he hadn't been particularly enamoured of Nigel Fontenoy. Abigail also knew now, after her conversation with Ben Appleyard, that it was more than that, much more than mere dislike: that Callaghan really had something to hate Nigel Fontenoy for. If any man had a reason for wishing Nigel Fontenoy off this planet, that man was Tom Callaghan. Moreover, he was a cold fish, and it was odds on that he wouldn't hesitate to stick the knife in, physically as well as metaphorically.

But there remained the matter of his alibi. He hadn't been at home that night. There was a girl, he said, a researcher on the programme, they'd had dinner straight after it finished, he'd stayed the night with her. Well, she'd be sure to confirm it. Callaghan would hardly have given her name, otherwise.

Callaghan had made himself some tea after the police had gone, and drank it standing in front of his big window, looking out at the distant hills, warming his hands round the mug. Standing here, the double glazing deadening any sound, he felt cut off, as if in a capsule that isolated him from any sensation outside himself, from anything other than the pain which walked beside him like his familiar, the incubus which had sat on his shoulder ever since Judy had died.

He'd known it would never go away until Nigel Fontenoy was dead, but now that he was, he saw how he'd fooled himself. The knowledge that his child had died, unnecessarily and before her time, would always be with him; it would be better if he, too, were dead. Yet the impulse to live was strong. Callaghan knew that he would never have the guts to take that way out. He wanted to live – and to live his life

111

in the way he chose. Which was not being locked up for the rest of it for killing Nigel Fontenoy.

Had it been a mistake to assume he could trust Claire Denton? To assume he needed her to lie for him? Even if he'd been alone with no alibi, what would that prove?

When it came to the crunch, it was every man, or woman, for themselves, and Claire was no exception; if pressure was put on her . . .

Well, he was more than capable of dealing with her or with anyone else who might see fit to put a spoke in his wheel.

15

George Fontenoy tried to shut his ears to the noise of the chainsaw and the shouts of the workmen demolishing what was left of the cedar. He kept away from the window, refusing to watch, or to give the crowd of sightseers a glimpse of himself, just something else to gawp at. Instead, he began to potter around, trying to do something about the residual mess left in his shop after the departure of the police Forensic team. Dust had infiltrated everywhere, even into the glass-topped counters; sooner or later they would have to be thoroughly cleaned out, but meanwhile, he saw no reason to endure the whitish, greasy fingerprint powder on his precious gems any longer. He began to work systematically on each piece with a camel-hair brush and a soft cloth, but his heart wasn't in it.

He was, by sheer effort of will, gradually accustoming himself to being where Nigel had been killed, since there was no question of closing down the shop for good, but for the moment he kept away from the office with its square of carpet missing from the centre.

He could have reopened now, had he been so inclined, but he'd decided to stay shut for the present, until he'd settled on a permanent course of action, although deep down, he knew what the end must be, that the decision had already been made for him. At his age, he probably had no choice but to continue along the path Nigel had begun, and sell out to Jermyn's, though the idea broke him up when he thought of it.

He dusted and rearranged a group of scent bottles, pretty glass trifles with jewelled stoppers, then stared into mid-air, the duster still clutched in one hand. Selling out? The idea was preposterous!

Picking up an elegant diamond brooch of the *belle époque*, he cradled it tenderly in the palm of his hand, working the soft brush expertly between the crevices, finishing off with a chamois leather to give it an extra lustre before laying it back on the dark blue velvet. It glittered expensively back at him, a confident, establishment piece, solidly encrusted; yet diamonds had never been his passion. Cold things, in his opinion, they lacked the warmth and depth of a fine ruby or emerald, or even the infinite variations of the semi-precious gemstones: milky striated moonstones, garnets and dragonfly-blue lapis, jade in all its variations, translucent chalcedonies, bloodstones green as seaweed, flecked with red . . . Their names formed a litany, a golden thread that had run throughout his life.

He'd always hoped that it would be Matthew who would continue the family succession – but Matthew had reacted violently to the suggestion implicit in Nigel's legacy to him, that he would take over where Nigel himself had left off. It had been a vain hope, George admitted now, both he and Nigel had been deluding themselves – though who could have predicted Nigel's untimely end, coming as it did before Matthew had had time to mature and settle down? As it was, he would certainly want to sell his share and squander everything on those damned cars he was so crazy about. Maybe it was better so. He'd no love or feel for the business, had only agreed to work here to cock a snook at his father.

Swallowing disappointment as bitter as bile, George lifted an Edwardian pendant, similar to the one which had disappeared, only of much better quality, a fine peridot in a platinum and diamond setting. He let it swing from his finger on its slender chain, gazing into its pale green fire, again puzzled as to why anyone should have taken the other, of less value, and in disrepair into the bargain. That, and the box.

Disaster and ill-luck had always seemed to hang over that box. Considering its provenance, that wasn't surprising. Why hadn't Nigel got rid of it, years ago, for what he could get?

The plain answer was that he'd been too avaricious, holding on too long, watching it accrue in value. An old failing that had cost them dear, more than once. George realized he wasn't being entirely fair to Nigel. Hadn't it simply been that he couldn't bear to part with it, incomplete as it was? He had loved beauty in all its forms. He had also been a perfectionist.

George had known, ever since that first moment when he had opened his eyes and seen the felled cedar lying on the ground, that what remained of his life would never be the same again. He'd been filled with a sense of fatalistic dread, which had never left him since. The tree's demise had been symbolic of the whole shambles left behind after Nigel's death. No longer was he going to be able to hide behind a pretence of not knowing what was going on.

Now, everything would be dragged out into the open. No facet of anybody's private life was considered private enough nowadays to be kept from the public gaze, especially when it involved murder. George was under no delusions that Nigel's death had its causes in his own actions. He had loved Nigel, but hadn't been blind to his faults. How much he'd been wounded over the years by the man his son had become, nobody but himself had known.

It was too much to ask of an old man. If he could have avoided the coming interview this afternoon with the young policewoman with the red hair, Inspector Moon, he would have done so. She was young, yes, but not inexperienced. She had clear, hazel eyes, and a direct look, which he tried to avoid without being too obvious about it. He had a feeling she saw too much.

George thought he might easily become very ill, if he allowed himself to be. Nigel, in the end, had paid the price, and for him, it was finished. It was the living who had to go on paying.

A new eating place had opened in Sheep Street. Once an old-fashioned shoe shop, then empty for a while, later taken over by Oxfam for a further period, it now called itself the Granary and had been refurbished, complete with Welsh dressers full of copper kitchen utensils and colourful plates, and corn dollies not looking as dusty yet as they soon would.

Abigail had arranged to meet Nan Randall there for coffee. 'And scones,' Nan requested, with a deep, throaty chuckle. 'Have to look after my figure, dear.'

Nan Randall, Mrs Herbert Petheridge in private life, would have been better advised to have left the scones alone. She was at least three stones overweight, bouncy as a rubber ball, but always impeccably and expensively dressed. Abigail had admired the eye-catching outfit she was wearing, which couldn't do much to minimize curves of that size, but gave her a definite pzazz. 'Thank you, love, though it should be my dressmaker you're admiring. Prezzie from my old man, when we went to our youngest's degree ceremony.'

Randy Nan, she'd been irreverently christened in her younger days, perhaps unfairly, perhaps not; but she'd put all that behind her long since, and married an extremely rich, amenable husband and now had three grown-up sons, hunky, rugby-playing extroverts all three. She was an extrovert herself, had worked for the *Advertiser* for thirty years, stopping only long enough to give birth. She was talkative, good-natured, very popular, had a long, journalistic memory, and a facility for getting people to talk to her.

'They're trying here, I'll give them that,' she said, looking around appraisingly as she tucked into excellent scones, noting the full tables with an approving nod. 'I'd have given them three months before I saw it, but maybe they'll stay the course. Yes, love, I covered that case. Harrowing, absolutely harrowing! I'd known Judy, you see . . . well, my Jason did – that's the one who has, by some amazing fluke, pulled off his degree. He used to bring her home, she was one of the gang he went around with, though when I say *knew* her, that's a figure of speech. She was so quiet you forgot she was there until you bumped into her. I was shocked, naturally, when she walked under that bus, but it's always the quiet ones, isn't it?'

'Do you know her father?'

Nan raised expressive eyebrows. 'Tom Callaghan? Only to salaam to, nowadays, when I meet him around town. Everybody's idol at the moment, isn't he?'

'Not mine,' Abigail said, sampling a scone before they all disappeared. 'And not yours, either, I'd guess.'

Nan contemplated the last scone, then pushed away her plate. 'I'd better not. I'm interviewing a captain of industry later on and he's giving me lunch afterwards. They know how to do themselves well, these tycoons, it'll be more than a plate of pasta at Gino's! No,' she added, spooning sugar heavily into her second cup of coffee, 'I don't like Callaghan. First met him when he came to work at the *Advertiser*, yonks ago, but I wouldn't say I knew him well, even then – or that anybody ever would. A deep one, that. Maybe where Judy got it from.'

'It must have been rotten for him, all the same, his daughter dying like that.'

'He was shattered! Well, both of them were, he and his wife. I hear she's left him, at last. They never got on, but she may've been pushed into going at last by Judy's death. They both doted on her, Callaghan especially. There didn't seem to be any reason for it, you know, she was doing all right at school, she was shy but she'd plenty of friends . . .'

'The verdict was accidental death, wasn't it?'

Nan gave her an old-fashioned look. 'One of the other girls in the gang, her best friend, told me afterwards that she'd had some sort of crush on an older man, but that didn't seem to be enough reason for her to have deliberately put herself in the way of being killed. All the same, when I heard dear Nigel had been murdered, it rang several bells. You never know what relevance these things have, do you?'

'What d'you mean by that – "dear Nigel"?'

Nan shrugged.

'Come on, tell me what you know about him.' Nan, for once, seemed reluctant, and Abigail pressed: 'He never married, did he?'

'No, but he wasn't gay, love, if that's what you're hinting.' Nan hesitated. 'Oh, what's it matter, he's dead . . . He liked women, yes, and the younger the better. No, not quite under age, but young enough. He was pathetic. It was all right when he was young, too, but he got older and never had a girlfriend over seventeen as far as I know.'

'Go on.'

'That's why I straight away believed young Sharon when she told me about Judy having a crush on him. I couldn't see him exactly discouraging her.'

Above the cornflower- and poppy-strewn café-style curtains two female heads appeared. Two pairs of eyes stared, embarrassingly close to the table where Abigail and Nan sat. Nan picked up the plate with the last scone and offered it. The two women looked indignant and moved away. Nan laughed.

'What do you know about Fontenoy's – the firm, that is?' Abigail asked.

'Oh, very OK, if you want expensive antique jewellery. Lovely things they have there. You pay for it, mind. They did once go in for modern stuff, custom designed, ages ago, just after we were married, I think, but it never seemed to get off the ground, though the girl who made it was pretty good. She'd won prizes, that sort of thing. I have a silver brooch somewhere,' Nan added carelessly. 'I'd have liked more, but when I inquired, she'd gone, and neither of the Fontenoys knew where to. Bertie bought me something else instead, so I didn't bother to follow it up. After she left, they went back to selling what they know best. Very wise.'

'Disappeared, did she? What was her name?'

'I don't know about disappeared – just left, I suppose.' Nan frowned in an effort to remember the name, last heard twenty-five years ago, mortified when it eluded her. Not being able to recall it instantly was a slur on her reputation as the longest memory on the *Advertiser*. 'Never mind, I'll remember it before the day's out and let you know. Or Ben will,' she added, gathering her things together. 'Hope I haven't said too much, it's a failing of mine. This one looks as though it might turn up some very nasty things and that touches all of us. I happen to be very fond of this town and I wouldn't want . . . Oh well, you know what I mean.'

She gave a slightly embarrassed laugh and sailed towards the door, Abigail in her wake. When they were parting to go their different ways, she said, 'Talking of Ben . . . I should make the most of him, if I were you; there's not enough on the *Advertiser* to keep him here long.'

There were worse towns to live in, Abigail supposed, thinking of what Nan Randall had said about Lavenstock, though having been born not far away, being so familiar with it, she'd largely taken it for granted, until as a policewoman she began to know it better, to know its darker side as well, its trouble spots, its depressed areas.

A market town of ancient lineage, with a minor public school, many fine old buildings, several venerable churches, and a swift river running through its lower reaches, it had a lot going for it. Surrounded by as yet unspoilt countryside, it encompassed within its boundaries some of the worst areas created during the Industrial Revolution, now sanitized beyond recognition. It had expanded to include numerous quiet villages on the outskirts. It had a bit of everything, really. Except an efficient one-way system, the present one being diabolical, and a regular subject of infuriated letters to the local paper.

'Thanks, but I need the exercise, it's good for the soul,' she'd said, refusing a lift from Pete Deeley across to Cedar House Antiques, where she was to meet Mayo. They'd lunched together in the Saracen's Head, using the time to discuss what her meeting with Nan Randall had revealed, and the substantial ploughman's lunch, one of their specials, plus the scone she'd eaten with Nan, needed to be worked off.

She walked briskly now from the lower town, the sun low in a greenish sky. It would be cold tomorrow. Only ten weeks to Christmas, proclaimed a toy shop window, already decorated with cotton wool snow and glitter that would be tatty weeks before then. They were putting up coloured lights at the entrance to the modern shopping precinct, too, which couldn't harm it and might even be an improvement. The precinct resembled the Taj Mahal on the outside, and inside had the same chain stores, stocking the same goods, to be found in every other precinct the length and breadth of the British Isles. Flanking the entrance was the new office development – half of the units still unlet – and the golden-windowed block where Wilding Enterprises hung out.

She'd still been thinking about Callaghan and this new aspect of his relationship with Fontenoy which had come up, but now, seeing Wilding's office, Jake Wilding's connections with the Fontenoys again occurred to her as she waited to cross at the traffic lights. Was there a link between Wilding as a suspect, and that missing box? Supposing the box to have contained papers, as Christine Wilding had suggested, and supposing them to have been incriminating to Jake . . .

But Nigel had taken the box to London, and inquiries about the train he had caught, the duration of his visit to Macaudle, and the time of his return to Lavenstock, suggested he'd had little time to go anywhere but Jermyn's, which had started one or two ideas of her own, none of them featuring the box being filled with papers, which Macaudle, when he returned, might be able to confirm.

The big clock on the ornate, newly restored, green-painted and gilded Victorian tower, standing cheerfully incongruous between the new hi-tech offices and the old, depressed library buildings, boomed the half hour. She crossed when the lights changed and took the short cut by the back of the parish church to Cedar House.

16

'Tea?' George asked, pooh-poohing the suggestion that it would be too much trouble. He served Earl Grey in beautiful, thin china cups which, however, owing to the shakiness of his hands, ended up with rather less than their full measure inside and too much outside in the saucer. Abigail thought he would have been wiser to have stayed with the Wildings at Ham Lane for the present. But no, he insisted, when she tactfully inquired, he was better back here in his own house, where he could be looked after by Mrs Anderson, his daily cleaning woman for over twenty years.

George, for his part, was relieved they didn't immediately start with the sort of questions he'd both anticipated, and dreaded. Having expected only the young woman, he was thrown off balance by the presence of her superior officer, though Mayo was keeping himself in the background, seemingly content to let her do the talking. He soon found it was himself who was doing the talking, however, though he was willing enough if it would put off the questioning. She had got him talking about the business, how the firm had started and how they operated. 'I'm surprised there's enough call in Lavenstock to support a family concern like yours,' the inspector had remarked. 'You're very specialized, aren't you?'

'In my grandfather's day, when he started the business, he didn't specialize at all, he simply sold fine jewellery, old or new. But there's too much rubbish sold nowadays – you don't generally find the quality you used to. But certainly we don't depend on local trade. We work through our catalogue and often with dealers.'

After that, launched into his favourite subject, the world he knew best, and his special interest in the Art Nouveau and *belle époque* styles, from the late nineteenth century to the Edwardian period just before the First World War, there was no stopping George. He even heard himself insisting they went through into the shop, to illustrate the points he was making.

Mayo, who had met George only briefly before, thought it wouldn't do to underestimate him: the flow of words, he guessed, was a smokescreen for something as yet not apparent. He was impressed, too, by the way he'd come to terms with his son's death; it seemed to Mayo that the old man was facing his bereavement with courage and dignity as well as practical common sense, not easy in any circumstances, let alone murder. He had tidied up the shop and already a new carpet covered the floor of the office where the bloodstained square had been cut out for forensic examination. Mayo's thrifty Yorkshire soul hoped that someone had remembered to tell him he could be compensated.

Wonderful period for designers, George was enthusing: Cartier, Boucheron, Tiffany, though none of them, in his opinion, was worthy to be mentioned in the same breath as Fabergé. Court jeweller to the Imperial Court of Russia before the terrible events of the revolution, he had worked in enamels and gold, precious and semi-precious stones, excelling in the creation of enamelled and gem-studded objects of vertu of the most delicate kind, restrained and elegant. Not to mention a whole series of marvellously carved hardstone animals, now fetching incredible prices.

'Oh yes, those beautiful jewelled eggs!' Abigail said.

'The Imperial Easter Eggs — you know about them?'

'There was an exhibition I saw . . . I remember one egg with a mechanical bird inside. Intriguing.'

'Oh, certainly. Most of them were designed as gifts from Tsar Nicholas II to the Tsarina Alexandra, and from Nicholas to his mother. But beautiful?' George's eyebrows lifted. 'Many of them were, yes. And the craftsmanship of them all is incomparable — but frankly, unlike his other pieces, some of them were hideously vulgar. One marvels at the expertise,' he remarked with a wry smile, 'but not the taste. If you want to see his most exquisite creations – ' He stopped, pulling himself up short. 'Never let an old man talk about his ruling passions!'

'Why not? I find it fascinating.' Abigail smiled, speaking with perfect truth. 'I've always admired that sort of thing – and Victorian jewellery.'

'I think you did once sell more modern stuff, though, individually designed?' Mayo put in, taking the cue.

George became at once very still. After a moment, he sat down on one of two chairs reserved for visitors and gestured to the other. Mayo nodded to Abigail to take it, and remained standing, arms folded, in the way he had, which perhaps he didn't know was forbidding. Yes, George admitted presently, they had, but it had been a mistake, and shut his mouth with an air of finality.

Mayo's expression warned Abigail to wait. They sat without speaking and a little clock somewhere ticked away several seconds before George gave in. 'It was a venture that didn't come off, unfortunately,' he said at last, with a small sigh. 'Nigel had the idea that selling original jewellery, taking individual commissions, would be a good idea.' The girl who made it, he added, was very young, but had had talent of a truly original sort, though that had been the trouble . . . Lavenstock wasn't ready for that sort of innovation. Or ready to pay the price, which had, perhaps, been more to the point. They understood and were willing to pay for a good diamond or sapphire which would keep its value, but not for experimental work which might date. The whole idea had been a disaster.

George spoke guardedly. He'd been led into this and was afraid of inadvertently revealing more than he should of what he had kept pushed down into the depths of his mind, until the murder had forced it to the surface. Since then, he'd been able to think of little else except that last terrible quarrel, of coming into the shop to intervene, standing in the doorway unobserved, and seeing Nigel with his hands round that delicate young throat. Nigel had seen him then and pushed the whimpering girl away and George had backed out, to his everlasting shame. The next morning, Nigel told him she'd left. For years George had had nightmares, wondering if he'd murdered her.

Just for a moment, he was strongly tempted to tell everything, but what would be gained by it? 'Who was she?' he asked, repeating the question that he realized Mayo had just put to him. Then, not being able to think of a reason for withholding that at least, he told them. The name meant nothing to either of them, yet.

'Why did she leave, Mr Fontenoy?' Mayo asked.

But George, deciding he'd said enough, took refuge in prevarication. 'Oh, I don't know, why do girls of that age do anything? No sense of purpose, no loyalty.'

'Was there a quarrel?'

The old man hum-ed and ha-ed and cleared his throat, looked anywhere but at his questioners, which Mayo took to mean yes.

'What was it about?'

'Bit of a misunderstanding, that's all, would've all blown over if she'd stayed. But no, they throw everything up the minute there's trouble, nowadays.'

'Mr Fontenoy, what was this quarrel about?'

'I don't know. Can't be expected to remember so far back, at my age . . .' Suddenly he clutched his chest, a contorted expression crossing his face. 'M'pills,' he gasped. 'Glass of water, please.'

You old rogue! Abigail thought as she rushed into the kitchen to get the water, you damned old rogue . . . Just when we were getting to the crunch. But don't you dare die on us yet, George! Because somebody knew the answers – some of them at any rate, and she'd bet she wasn't far out in thinking that could be George Fontenoy.

He recovered, as she'd known he would, with amazing rapidity, but they stayed with him until they were sure it was safe to leave him in the care of Mrs Anderson, summoned by telephone from her house round the corner. There was no question of any further interrogation.

Abigail gave a last frustrated look at Cedar Antiques as she

124

got into Mayo's car. He negotiated it into the stream of traffic, then, when they were clear, he asked soberly, 'Why am I getting such a sense of urgency about this case? A feeling that somebody has left some unfinished business?'

It was as near to admitting a premonition as she'd ever known from Mayo, and it struck chill in her heart. The implication that an undiscovered killer might still be at large, might even be prepared to kill again, wasn't something to contemplate with comfort.

'Should he be left alone there? Wouldn't he be better back with the Wildings?' she asked, and then felt a further chill as, simultaneously, the thought occurred to her that the old man might not, in fact, be much safer there. If the murder had originated from one of the suspects living at Ham Lane, it would be a simple matter, supposing George to represent any threat, to get rid of him, to stage an accident. To push him so that he pitched headlong down a flight of stairs, say, and broke his neck. She shivered.

'Oh, that's all right. I had a word with Mrs Anderson in the kitchen. It seems her son's a full-back with Lavenstock Lions, and she's promised to get him to sleep in until further notice.'

Why didn't I think of that? wondered Abigail. And, having stirred up her apprehensions, why did he now make her feel as though she was being foolishly over-cautious?

She wasn't to know that Mayo's thoughts had been momentarily distracted by catching a glimpse, as they passed the end of the street, of the interior decorating shop belonging to Alex's sister, Lois French, closed while she was away. She was looking for a new partner and finding it difficult to settle on anyone since the one she really wanted was Alex, to which end she'd been pursuing a relentlessly wearing-down process for some time now. Alex wasn't a person easy to wear down, as Mayo knew to his cost, but Lois had had plenty of opportunity while they'd been away together, while Alex was in a very vulnerable state. His hands tightened on the wheel and then he put his private life firmly back in its own compartment.

*　　　*　　　*

Since that shocking day when her best friend had walked under a bus, when they were both sixteen, still at school and going around in a gang, Sharon Wallace had done some growing up. Now a smooth and sophisticated twenty-one, she worked in PR at the nearby television centre, had her own flat, drove a red Fiesta and had her straight, short hair tinted a rich mahogany, sculpted and cut to curve under at the ends and fall across one eye.

Jenny Platt had been detailed to interview her and had made an appointment to meet her at home, after work. Arriving a little early, she sat in her car outside the block of flats until she saw a young woman drive up, guessed who she was and waited until she'd had time to get indoors before following and ringing her bell.

Sharon had slipped off her shoes, but hadn't yet had time to change and was still wearing the white suit and emerald shirt she'd worn to work. She poured gin and tonic on to ice for herself, the same for Jenny, without the gin. Not a young woman to lack confidence on the face of things, she was, for some reason, very nervous.

'Why do you want to talk about Judy? She's been dead six years!'

'It could have a bearing on some other inquiries we're making. We thought you'd remember her death and might help us.'

Sharon's eyes clouded. 'How could I ever forget? She was my best friend, we did everything together! Of course I'll help. I've put flowers on the railings near the spot where she died every year since then.'

'That's nice,' smiled Jenny, whose own 'best friend' days were not too far behind. 'But there must have been some things you didn't share. One or two secrets.'

'None that matter, now.'

'You told Nan Randall – Mrs Petheridge – you thought she was seeing an older man,' Jenny prompted. 'Did Judy tell you who it was?'

The ice-cubes clinked against the sides of her glass as Sharon swirled it around. The wing of her hair fell forward, obscuring her face as she bent her head. She had pale skin and wore a lot of dark lipstick. When she looked up, her lower lip was trembling and her big brown eyes were full of tears.

'I told her she was playing with fire. She wouldn't say who it was, not in so many words.'

'What gave you the idea it was Nigel Fontenoy?'

'Nigel Fontenoy?' Sharon veered like a startled horse, then met the sympathetic yet adamant face of the young policewoman. She hesitated. After a moment, she said, 'Well, she came to the school dance, wearing what she said was an antique bracelet . . . I mean, you had to believe it was the real thing, sparkly stuff and little pearls and everything, not the sort of jewellery any of us could afford, even if we'd wanted it. I thought maybe it was her mother's, that she'd lent it to her, but she said no and went all mysterious. After that, I just sort of put two and two together and guessed who'd given it to her – which turned out to be a big mistake.'

'A mistake? You guessed the wrong person?'

'No, no! It was just that Judy was very quiet, you know, and a bit shy, she didn't have any boyfriends. She had to be making it up, hadn't she, just so we wouldn't pity her?'

'That's possible. Sharon, how do you account for the way she died?'

'It was an accident, they said so at the inquest! She just crossed the road without looking!' Sharon was becoming very agitated. She was still very young under the thin veneer of sophistication.

'You didn't think it was an accident at the time, though, did you? You told Mrs Petheridge why you thought she'd done it.'

'I was over-reacting and imagining things!'

Jenny said, 'Where did you think she got the bracelet, then?'

'Maybe her parents bought it for her, in spite of what she said. Her father used to spoil her rotten, but he said no, they hadn't, and that they hadn't found it among her things after she –' She broke off. 'It's because Nigel Fontenoy's been murdered, isn't it? That's why you're asking all these questions – that's why –'

'Her father told you that?' Jenny interrupted. 'When?'

'Oh, recently. About a month ago, I suppose. It was the first time I'd seen him since Judy died.'

'How did you come to be discussing this? Had he specifically arranged to meet you and talk about it?'

Sharon stared at her. 'Judy's dad? Good heavens, no! He's *Tom Callaghan*, didn't you know? We just happened to bump into each other when I was trying to start my old car one night after work, only it wouldn't. I've got a new one now. He was coming out of the TV centre and had a look at it. He said I was wasting my time trying to start it and offered me a lift home. He's really great, isn't he?' she asked, dazzled by fame and a smooth tongue. 'He suggested stopping off for something to eat and asked me if I'd join him. We had a bottle of wine and, well . . .'

'You began to talk about Judy?'

Colour rushed up under the pale, polished make-up. 'He was the one who first mentioned her, not me! I mean, I'd have been scared of upsetting him, but he said it helped to talk about her. He asked me if I really believed she'd commit suicide and I said no, not now, though I had at first. And I told him why.'

'What was his reaction?'

'He was very nice about it, but he agreed with me that I'd been reading too much into things. He said Nigel Fontenoy was a family friend and agreed there was no way Judy would've killed herself, and that she must have made up the story about the bracelet.'

'Where do you think she got it, then – and what's happened to it? If her parents don't have it, who does?' Sharon's big brown eyes were troubled. 'You have it, don't you?' Jenny asked, gently.

'She – she asked me to look after it for her when she wasn't wearing it because she didn't want her parents to see it.'

'May I see it?'

'I haven't got it now. Her father asked me for it . . . I didn't want it, anyway, reminding me of Judy every time I looked at it.'

17

Carmody poked his head round Abigail's office door, waving papers, looking so like a bloodhound that had got the scent that she couldn't forbear to smile. 'From Forensics, and about time,' he announced. 'Knew you'd want to see it straight away.'

She swallowed the last of the warm croissant she'd picked up at Selina's Sarnies round the corner by way of breakfast, drained her coffee and put aside Jenny Platt's report, which opened up interesting speculations about Tom Callaghan's involvement in Fontenoy's murder. She'd done a good job there, and was now on her way to see the woman Callaghan alleged he'd spent the night with, for what it was worth. A good girl, Jenny, dependable, tough as old boots under that innocent face and mop of curls – and shrewd. As she'd pointed out, with the revelations about the bracelet, Callaghan had more than enough to convince him that Judy had in some way been secretly associating with Nigel. Add to that the fact that Nigel was old enough to be her father, and claimed to be one of Callaghan's best friends – well, any father would have felt like killing Fontenoy.

Abigail picked up the papers Carmody had left with her, pushing aside a couple of bulky files on her desk to make more room. Surrounded by computers as they were, it was a constant source of wonderment to her why the stacks of paper never seemed to lessen. After she'd read the report through and absorbed the information it contained, she scooped it up and took it in to Mayo.

'So it *was* blood in the truck, Abigail.'

'Well, yes,' she said doubtfully. No doubt about it, the stain

Carmody had seen was blood, human blood, but Group O – the group to which Nigel Fontenoy had belonged – along with Abigail Moon and half the CID and a fair percentage of the rest of the population. 'But it'll take weeks to complete a full DNA probe.' And yet, if the analysis turned out to be positive, it would show that this particular blood had only about a one in eight million chance of *not* being that of Nigel Fontenoy.

'Life's too short to let that hold us up,' Mayo decided. 'For the time being, we've enough supporting evidence to proceed on the reasonable assumption that it was Jake Wilding's truck which transported Fontenoy's body to Nailers' Yard. Hair and fibres from his clothing found in the truck, plus the gravel extracted from the grazes on his face – which I see Dexter says comprises brick dust and cement.'

'You'll also see they found minute traces of soil in Fontenoy's office. Red, sandy. The same soil as that on Wilding's building site. It looks as though Fontenoy *was* stabbed there in the office.'

Mayo went on to read the rest of the report. The square of carpet which had been removed hadn't yielded sufficient uncontaminated blood to be of use, but the SOCO team had uncovered a further identical type bloodstain on the A4 pad on his desk, one spot which hadn't been noticed by the murderer, because it had fallen directly upon the ink stain which had been soaking through the pad. The killer, carefully cleaning up the office, even to the extent of neatly recapping Fontenoy's gold fountain pen and cleaning the carpet with biological detergent, the sort guaranteed to remove oil, egg, blood, sweat (and even toil and tears, who could tell?) had missed that stain, masked as it was by the ink.

Mayo looked up, frowning. 'Don't you find that odd, Abigail? Somebody as meticulous as that neglecting to clean up the blood on the bottom of the pick-up? Unless he was disturbed, and couldn't get back to it.' If, for instance, the truck had been "borrowed" by someone.

'Or unless he was incredibly confident that the bloodstains would never be recognized as such – and certain that the truck would never be connected with the murder, anyway.'

An assumption the killer might have got away with, too, all things being equal . . .

'There's something else you ought to know about friend Wilding. We've been checking his alibi, and guess what we found?'

Mayo wanted to talk to Jake Wilding himself, but it was early evening before they were able to go up to Ham Lane once more.

Abigail drove, to the accompaniment of a sad little piece by Ravel in a minor key, emanating from Mayo's radio, permanently tuned to Radio 3. Classic FM, interspersed with adverts, he scorned as upmarket wallpaper music. Serious music was an occupational hazard when driving with Mayo. He claimed it helped to oil the workings of his brain, which was why he preferred to close his eyes and let someone else take the wheel.

October was well advanced and although the clocks hadn't yet gone back it was rapidly growing dark. The long, dry summer and the big storm had completed an early leaf fall, and the trees were bare-branched against the darkening sky. Boys were knocking the few remaining conkers from the horse chestnuts outside the park gates. There was a strong nip in the air, a sparkle of frost on the tarmac, a foretaste of winter.

The two Wildings and Callaghan, Mayo was thinking behind closed lids. Matthew Wilding, who had the carrot of a promised inheritance from Fontenoy as motive, but who had allegedly been drunk and incapable that night. Young, immature, but murderously inclined? Debatable. And his father, against whom the evidence was steadily piling up, his motive so far unclear, unless it was to rid himself of the debt he owed to his cousin. It wasn't a motive Mayo was inclined to give credence to. And was Wilding the sort to be capable of this murder? Mayo could see Jake using his fists, or even the traditional blunt instrument, but a stiletto? Wasn't there something a bit too subtle about that for Jake? On the other hand, if it had simply been there, when a quarrel arose . . .

His prospects, however you looked at it, were less than happy.

And now Callaghan, who had a significant grudge against Fontenoy but against whom there was as yet no evidence whatsoever to prove he'd actually gone so far as to murder him. But it didn't take much imagination to see him sliding a knife into soft flesh.

For the moment, however, the main focus must remain on Wilding, at present at home and in the bosom of his family. An inconvenient time to call, suppertime, but Mayo was making no excuses for a strategy designed to catch them all at their ease, and hopefully off guard.

A figure was straddling a heavy motorbike as they drove up to the house, bending over the side to adjust something. 'Thought it was cars, not motorbikes, Matthew Wilding was interested in,' he remarked, opening his eyes on the scene.

But it wasn't Matthew. The raven black hair was as long as a girl's, and as the person sat up and pulled on a crash helmet, they saw it was in fact a girl. And Abigail saw a face that kept her immobile, that impressed itself on her retina, an unforgettable face, olive-skinned, with a very straight nose, full lips and smouldering eyes, a face full of drama and self-will. Before the car had stopped, the rider had kicked the machine into life and roared down the drive.

'Maybe it's the daughter. Christine Wilding's.'

'Whoever she is, she can handle that bike better than most men.'

But Christine's daughter proved to be with the rest of the family. Matthew was there, too, although he had his own flat over the old stables. She was a small, silent, grave-faced girl with a slightly fey quality about her who was introduced as Lindsay Hammond, the girl who had confirmed that Matthew had arrived home at about eleven on the night of Fontenoy's murder. She had straight brown hair and big grey eyes and was wearing a thick, cream Arran sweater, as if she were cold, though the heating was switched on and the flames of a cheerful fire were licking up the chimney, their light reflecting on the glowing bronzes. Matthew, on the other hand, was wearing sweat pants and a short-sleeved

T-shirt that revealed muscular arms. He looked less than pleased to see them but had lost that air of desperation he'd had when they'd first talked to him.

The family had just finished an early meal. 'We were about to have coffee, will you join us?' Christine offered politely.

'Thank you, that would be nice.'

'I'll get it,' Lindsay said, and disappeared, to reappear with a tray only a few moments later. Outwardly cool and composed as she poured the coffee with neat, economical movements, yet she seemed tense and withdrawn, giving an impression that she had erected an invisible barrier around herself plainly saying 'Keep Out'.

As for Wilding himself, he seemed quite unworried, looking relaxed and casual in a soft tan cashmere sweater and slacks, totally in command of himself, central to the situation. A hard man to upstage, he would enjoy being the focus of attention. There was a vitality about him, even sitting relaxed, with his long legs outstretched, that made everyone else seem lethargic, though Christine Wilding wasn't a woman to be overlooked by any standards, and this second marriage had all the outward appearances of a successful partnership. For all his confident manner, Jake Wilding often looked at his wife before he spoke. Abigail sensed a strong bond, stronger than they were perhaps aware of. And wondered again at the misery she'd seen in Christine's eyes when she had arrived at the shop on the morning after the murder.

Mayo didn't waste any time. 'I'd like to check over your statement, Mr Wilding. You said you arrived to see Mr Fontenoy at ten p.m.?'

'I've already told you all this – but all right, if you must. Yes, I got there at ten and stayed with him for about an hour – I think it was an hour but I can't be sure.'

'And got home, as Mrs Wilding confirmed, at quarter past eleven?'

'Actually, we made a slight mistake about that. It may've been later, probably nearer midnight, or just after.'

Although he said 'we', there was no agreement from his wife, who stared into the fire, her extraordinary turquoise eyes luminous in its light, her hair a vibrant fall of copper around her face.

'Midnight, then,' Mayo repeated. 'I see. And what were you doing in between?'

'It'd escaped my mind when I spoke to you earlier that I'd called in at my office, my main office in Chandlers' Way, on the way home. Sorry about that.' Wilding's smile was all-encompassing, an easy smile which anticipated no trouble, though he must have known his alleged forgetfulness was a blatant fabrication which wouldn't deceive a soul, let alone a couple of police officers who could spot a lie at fifty paces.

'Any particular reason for going back there at that time of night?'

'I wanted to be alone for a while to think about what Nigel and I had been discussing.'

'That would be the matter of the loan?'

An impatient expression crossed Wilding's face. 'Oh yes, the loan. Yes, that was it.'

Like hell it was, thought Mayo. It was something more than that. 'And you sat there for nearly an hour, thinking it over?'

'It took some thinking about. There were . . . conditions.'

'What conditions?'

'I'm sorry, I don't see that has any bearing on what happened to Nigel.'

'I wouldn't be asking if I didn't think it had.'

'Look, I've told you what you wanted to know, where I was, what more do you want?'

Mayo gave the man a hard stare, seemed about to press him, then tried another tack. 'Is there anyone who can verify what you've just said? Did anybody see you there at your office?'

'The security man. He'll tell you what time I got there. I believe we exchanged some remarks about the storm getting up.'

'And he can also confirm what time you left?'

'I'm not sure about that. I think he was on his rounds then, which didn't matter, as far as I was concerned. Naturally, I've the means of getting in and out of my own premises – and I've said what time I got home.'

'I have to tell you, we've already spoken to the security man and he confirms your call at the office. But he also says it wasn't much after eleven-twenty, when he was coming back into the foyer after visiting the toilet, that he saw you leaving,' Mayo said, keeping his private opinions of the so-called security arrangements at Wilding Enterprises to himself. 'I reckon it's about a ten-minute drive from Chandlers' Way to here.'

'*You've been checking up on me with my office?*'

'Oh yes, sir, matter of routine.' It was easier to fall back on police-speak than to explain the obvious, that *every* statement was painstakingly checked.

Jake's brows came down, thunderclouds appeared on the horizon. The room held its breath, and everyone in it held theirs. Christine's hands were tightly clasped together. Then Wilding smiled and the sun shone again. 'Of course, you would do that.'

Mayo exchanged a glance with Abigail. It had been a fair performance, a good pretence of anger, but it wouldn't wash. Wilding had already been perfectly aware, before he was told, that the police had been checking with his security people, otherwise, why had he so prudently amended his statement?

He now said easily, 'Well then, the security man must've been mistaken, mustn't he?'

'During the storm, Mr Wilding, a large branch fell off a tree in your neighbours' garden and smashed through their greenhouse roof. They were awake because of this and Mr Blamey and his wife both say they saw your car drive past their house and into the drive. But that was nearly one o'clock, not half past eleven.'

'What?' Wilding was taken aback, as well he might be if he hadn't known until then that his neighbours had been questioned about movements in his household that night, and furious for real, this time, though he tried to conceal it. He really had a temper, this man. Mayo noted it with interest.

Matthew, who had been exhibiting signs of boredom, shift-

135

ing restlessly on his seat throughout this conversation, suddenly jumped up, too, declaring, 'I'm off, you don't want me here.'

'Stay where you are, Matthew,' his father snapped. Matthew looked pretty sick but, after a moment's hesitation, sat down again, scowling.

'We'd better have the rest of it, Mr Wilding. Where did you go between leaving your office at eleven-twenty and getting home just before one?' Receiving no reply, Mayo pressed, 'Maybe you went up to your building site, to check that everything was all right?'

Jake gave a sudden, unamused laugh. 'So that's where these questions are leading! I might've known. Oh yes – I'm well aware certain sections of the community believe I was responsible for knocking down Forde Manor. I can't tell you how bloody stupid that idea is.'

'You're saying it wouldn't have been possible?'

'Oh, it's possible all right, but that site's potentially worth a packet to me. The manor house was a listed building. If it was proved that I'd deliberately demolished it, d'you think I'd ever be allowed to develop the site?'

'I couldn't comment on that. Out of my province. But there's plenty of evidence to show it didn't fall down on its own – smashed fences, vehicle tracks leading to and from your site. Until it's proved otherwise, it's bound to be assumed you had a hand in it.'

'You're making my point – if I *had* knocked it down, I'd have made bloody certain there wasn't any evidence left!'

Yes, I dare say you'd have tried, Mayo thought, having seen no reason as yet to revise Carmody's opinion of Wilding as a slippery customer. 'Then if you didn't go along to the site after you left your office, where were you, sir, for the next hour and a half?'

'Since I don't see that's any of your damned business, I don't propose to tell you.'

'Think about it, Mr Wilding. I'd advise you to think carefully about your position.'

Wilding crossed to a drinks table in the corner to pour himself a large slug of neat Scotch, downing half of it in a gulp. Christine said in a low voice, 'Oh, tell them, Jake, tell them. It doesn't really matter, whatever it is.' Their eyes met, as if there was nobody else in the room. It was a woman, Abigail thought.

'Was it a woman you were visiting?' Mayo asked. It usually was. 'And before you say anything, I have to tell you that we've examined the pick-up truck belonging to you, and found forensic evidence indicating that Nigel Fontenoy's body was at some time transported in it.'

Wilding was beginning to look hunted. His gaze travelled round the circle of faces. Either way he was in a cleft stick: if he didn't tell the truth about where he'd been he ran the risk of laying himself open either to suspicion of knocking down the house, or much worse, murder. If he did . . . The silence lengthened. He finished his whisky. 'All right. But it isn't what you think.'

If I'd a pound for every time I'd heard that, thought Mayo, I could retire tomorrow.

Abigail said nothing either, but waited, her pencil at the ready. Wilding suddenly took hold of his wife's hand and, eventually, spoke. 'It was my ex-wife I went to see.' And was silent again.

'Her name and address, sir?' Abigail prompted, unaware of the havoc she was wreaking.

'Mrs Naomi Graham.' Wilding gave her address, which Abigail copied down, while his wife and their children looked on in varying degrees of stunned disbelief.

The Black Bull wasn't the sort of place Mayo would have put a foot in by choice, but tonight it would serve its purpose, which was as a convenient place to have a drink with Abigail and talk over the latest events before going home. It was pretty insalubrious, its air thick with tobacco fumes, its ceilings pickled dark brown, with a noisy darts match in progress, a juke-box playing non-stop, and video-games along one wall, but there were quiet corners. In any case, you could probably have shouted state secrets at the top of your voice and not been heard over the noise.

The first person they saw on entering was Carmody. He

went to get them drinks, and while Abigail was in the ladies, Mayo hitched himself into a corner bench seat by the window, abstractedly watching the darts players. He was thinking how aptly it had all slotted into place after Jake Wilding had given them the name of his ex-wife. Naomi Graham. The name George Fontenoy had supplied, the young jewellery designer who had worked briefly with the Fontenoys, disappeared and then, it now transpired, re-appeared later to marry Jake Wilding and give birth to Matthew. A brief interlude, after which she'd once more departed, leaving her child behind. And had recently re-turned to Lavenstock yet again, this time plus a daughter – and another son, older than Matthew by several years.

'I should never have gone to see her. She's always been big trouble,' Wilding had admitted bitterly. 'I should've told Nigel to go to hell when he asked me, let him do his own dirty work, then I wouldn't have been in this mess.'

'And you expect us to believe that's the only reason you went to see her – simply because Nigel Fontenoy asked you to?'

'I owed him one, I felt it was the least I could do.'

Something about the way he said that made Mayo think again about the contents of the letter Nigel Fontenoy had written to Wilding. And he thought he knew what was wrong about that idea of a loan. 'To repay what you owe me,' was how Fontenoy had phrased it. Nothing about repay-ment of *money*. 'We're talking other kinds of favours here, I take it, not hard cash? It wasn't the repayment of a loan you went to discuss with him?'

'I've never said it was. It was you jumped to that con-clusion yourselves. I did owe Nigel a bob or two, sure, but that wasn't why I finally agreed to help him. He'd been very useful to me, not long ago, and I don't forget things like that.'

Nor, apparently, did Fontenoy, and hadn't been averse to reminding Wilding of the fact. Favours in kind, thought Mayo. Blackmail was another word for it. Either was a lot more credible than the idea of Fontenoy having the sort of big money Wilding would be interested in borrowing.

'All right, tell me in what way you were obligated to him.'

But Wilding wouldn't be pushed that far. 'Never mind, it was nothing to do with this business.'

'I suggest it had everything to do with it. It was Fontenoy you owed, and Fontenoy who was murdered. Don't tell me you'd have run errands for him on a night like that if you'd been able to get out of it.'

'Running errands wasn't how I saw it. The storm didn't really get all that bad until after midnight – and anyway, there was something personal I needed to discuss with Naomi – something she'd written to me about.' Wilding had glanced uneasily at Matthew, who had been sitting in frozen silence during these revelations. The glance lingered for a moment before he turned deliberately away, avoiding looking at the boy. 'She has her elder son living with her. She seems to have some crazy idea in her head that he's my son, too.'

Carmody, followed by Abigail, came back from the bar with a half of shandy and a Scotch, putting the former in front of Abigail.

'Cheers, Ted.'

'Well, did he knock that house down? Wilding, I mean?'

'If he didn't,' Mayo said, 'he could know who did. A back-hander to one of his workmen, it's been done before. It's part of the pattern, though I'm damned if I see how, just yet.'

He sipped his Bell's, not to his taste but the best whisky on offer here, and relapsed into silence. Carmody, listening to Abigail give the gist of the interview, regretfully contemplated the froth left on the sides of his glass, all that was left of his beer. He was driving home and two halves was his limit. 'And you thought the Book of Genesis was complicated,' was his comment on the Wilding family relationships.

'It changes things,' Abigail said. 'At least we know now what it was Fontenoy expected Wilding could get from Naomi that he couldn't – some sort of document or letter is what he says. Wilding swears she wouldn't, in fact, give it to him, though Fontenoy must've thought Wilding had it in his power to make her an offer she couldn't refuse for it. But whatever that might've been, he isn't saying.'

'A promise to acknowledge Joss Graham as his son?' Carmody suggested. 'Wilding might have agreed to that – might even have been glad to find an heir to his business, since Matthew doesn't appear to be interested.'

The silence that greeted this didn't encourage him to go on.

Mayo said, 'Somebody should go and see this Naomi Graham. I think it ought to be you, Abigail. From all we've heard, anyone in trousers is likely to be eaten alive.'

'I'll go first thing tomorrow.' She frowned. 'You know, I find it hard to believe that Wilding really didn't know who Joss Graham was until he got that letter from Naomi.'

Mayo wasn't so sure. 'No reason why he should connect everyone he met by the name of Graham with his ex-wife, is there? Especially if he never knew Naomi had had a child before she married him, as he claims – though why she never told him, if she thought he was the father, beats me.' He took a sip of his whisky. 'And it was fairly obvious from the way both young Matthew and Lindsay Hammond took the news that they'd no idea of any family connections.'

'I'm having problems with that,' Abigail said, pushing her chair back and preparing to leave. She still had at least an hour's work in front of her at the station, and then the drive home before she could drop thankfully into bed. That was what her life seemed to consist of lately – work and bed. Too much of one and not enough of the other. She stifled a cracking yawn. 'No, I can't imagine being friends with people for as long as they have, and not knowing the first thing about them.'

'I can,' said Carmody, who had three children of his own, now dispersed about the country in various jobs and universities, whom he only saw when they came home for Maureen to do their washing. Quite often, they didn't know their friends' surnames and sometimes, he suspected, not even their forenames, since whatever their mothers had had them christened, they all seemed to answer to nicknames consisting of grunts of one syllable.

18

Lindsay couldn't, however hard she tried, ever remember a more dread evening. As far as she was concerned, scenes of any kind were to be avoided at all costs. Family scenes were even worse. And when they happened in front of other people – in this case the police – they were the absolute pits.

She woke the next morning feeling worse than if she hadn't gone to bed at all. Her eyes flew open and she was instantly fully awake, every gruesome detail of the night before clear and sharp in her mind, intensifying and adding an extra edge to the misery of the last days. She'd begun to feel so much more as if she were getting a grip back on reality over the last few weeks, almost back to her normal self, and then Nigel had been murdered, and everything had fallen apart again. All her life she'd been plagued by too much imagination and her sleep last night had been filled with dark dreams.

She could smell freshly brewed coffee and grilled bacon, hear Jake moving about, getting ready for work. How could they? How could they act normally, just as if nothing had happened!

Her clothes, usually neatly folded the night before, lay thrown anyhow over a chair. She washed hurriedly, scrambled into jeans and sweater, went downstairs and poked her head round the kitchen door. Matthew was there, leaning against the cupboards, a steaming mug of coffee in his hand. He looked ghastly, waxy pale under his tan, like old chewing gum. Her mother sat at the table, also drinking coffee. Lindsay was even more shocked at her haggard appearance, though she was already dressed, in a polo-necked green sweater and corduroy trousers, and was even made up, which was a mistake.

'I'm going for a swim,' Lindsay announced.

'Watch you don't get cold. It's a chilly morning. Don't forget to dry your hair properly.'

'Mum!'

'I'll see she does as she's told. I'll come with you, Lin.' Matthew finished his coffee in one swig and added with uncharacteristic meekness, 'If you don't mind.'

Once in the conservatory, he dived into a cubicle and emerged a minute or two later, wearing his trunks, to find Lindsay still dressed, sitting on the edge of the pool with her arms round her knees. 'Aren't you coming in?'

'No, I just wanted to get out of the house. I couldn't handle a repeat of last night's heavy performance.'

'Add me to that! But now I'm here, I'm going in.'

He slipped cleanly into the blue water and swam down the length of the pool in a swift, powerful crawl. Matthew, an intensely physical person, was in his element in the water. Once in, he could be counted on to stay there for half an hour at least. Lindsay got up and went to make herself a cup of instant coffee at the bar in the corner, where basic facilities had been installed for the purpose, and took it back to the side of the pool. She didn't really approve of the extravagant waste of resources needed to heat the building and the water, but it was comforting in here, with all the light and colour and a relaxing, steamy warmth that encouraged the exuberant growth of the conservatory plants Christine had brought in, though she disliked that over-sweet, cloying smell from some white-flowered plant or other which climbed to the roof. She sipped her coffee, which she'd made double strength in the hope that it might kick her into life, and watched Matthew's arms punching in and out of the water as if it were an enemy he was fighting.

She suddenly felt sorrier for him than for herself. If it had been bad for her last night, how much worse it must have been for him. To discover, at one blow, that people you'd only just got to know, really, were your half-brother and half-sister – and that *Naomi* was your mother! No wonder he'd freaked out.

His violent and incoherent denials, after his initial shocked silence, seemed to have been echoing in her head all night: 'She's not my mother! I haven't got a mother. She left me when I was eight months old!'

Poor Matthew. But like it or not, he was going to have to accept it, and that Naomi was Jake's alibi for the night Nigel had been murdered.

He finished several punishing lengths and then pulled himself out of the water and sat dripping beside her. 'More coffee?' He shook his head. Despite the breadth of his shoulders, his hairy chest and the faint shadow round his jawline due to not having shaved that morning, he looked like a small boy desperately needing comfort. But she didn't know how to give it, even if worries of her own hadn't been crowding in on her.

He ran his hands through his short, crisp hair, scything the water from it, and sat in a dejected posture, his feet dangling. 'What a mess, Lin. What a bloody, awful mess I've made of everything.'

'*You*'ve made a mess? Sure you don't mean your father?'

'My father! Oh, yeah, him, too. Must run in the family. Poor old Dad! Imagine being married to *that woman* –' His shoulders hunched. 'D'you think Joss might be his, really? I know what he said but I mean, he did know her before and she seems to have put it about a bit in her younger days.' He wanted to be as cruel as he could, not troubling to conceal his contempt of Naomi when he spoke. It was going to take something drastic for him to admit to her as his mother. 'She's weird. No wonder they're like they are.'

'But I thought you liked them – Joss and Cassie?'

'Well, I do. They're all right . . . they're different, I suppose. But I don't want either of them for a brother and sister.'

She knew exactly what he meant.

He sat curled into an uncomfortable-looking, almost foetal position, his knees up, his hands clasping his feet, his head down between his knees, like some Indian yogi. Avoiding looking at her, he suddenly began talking. 'I've been pissed off with Dad for months, but I'm sorry now I've given him such a hard time . . . I only took the job with Nigel to spite him because he was so bloody-minded about the rallying. And about me not going into the firm with him.'

Lindsay wondered just how important the rally driving was to him. Hadn't it occurred to him that before long he'd have Nigel's money, and there'd be nothing to prevent him? She caught her breath. A thought occurred to her, so unacceptable that she pushed it immediately away.

'Let's face it,' he was going on, 'he can be a right bastard when you don't spring to attention . . . but lately . . . Jeez, I don't know, I've wanted to stop it but somehow I couldn't. You know how it is, you take up an attitude and there's no back-tracking without looking stupid?'

'No,' said Lindsay, clear-eyed and positive. She simply could not see any point in holding on to a situation like that, just through pride, or from fear of losing face. Perhaps men looked at it differently. Then it struck her that maybe it wasn't as clear cut as all that, that maybe she, too –

Matthew was speaking again, and suddenly, as what he was saying got to her, she began to feel very frightened.

'And now . . . I only wanted to . . . God, Lin, what have I done?'

He'd begun to shake. Lindsay's blood ran cold. Terrified of what he was going to say next, she scrambled to her feet. 'Don't tell me any more! I don't want to hear! I've done enough for you already and I've too many troubles of my own. I'm sorry, Matthew!'

And with that, she fled, back to the house, up to her room, on to her bed, where she lay face down until the panic and shame at herself had subsided. Calmer after a while, she sat up and reached out, almost blindly, for her little morocco jewellery box, lifting out the inset tray. Underneath was the flat box containing the first object she'd received. And now also, the heavy intaglio seal ring, too big for her slender fingers. Half frightened, she slipped it on to her thumb and gazed at it for a long time, as if she could will herself to be less uneasy with it: at the lapis-lazuli centre, the deep, intense blue of a butterfly's wing, finely incised with the face of the god Janus, looking both ways. It glowed with a rather sinister light, and as she looked, she knew with a panicky feeling that she'd no choice, really, but to listen to Matthew, however awful what he had to tell her was: she had to help him, whatever he'd done. Her whole self shrank from it but she recognized his dangerous mood and was, quite simply, terrified of what he might do next.

She bundled the jewellery back anyhow into the box and ran down the stairs. In her agitation, she failed to notice that the seal ring, snatched from her thumb, had fallen off the dressing table and rolled into a corner as she ran out of the room.

And when she reached the conservatory again, Matthew had disappeared.

It was raining when Abigail woke up. Seriously, with no immediate prospect of giving up. She hadn't slept well and after making a hurried breakfast of tea and toast, left the cottage still feeling heavy-eyed and despondent, as if in tune with the weather.

She met the post van at the bottom of her lane. Leaning out of the window to take her mail from the cheery postman, she waved to a figure she thought was the female Fossdyke, shut the window before Fido could push his slavering snout in and threw the bundle of letters on to the seat beside her until she'd drawn up in the station car park. A quick flick through revealed a couple of bills, charity circulars, a letter from a school friend, and a shiny postcard of a despondent frog contemplating a leap up to a mile-high lily pad. *When are we going to climb that hill behind your cottage? There's a wonderful view from the top,* she read. The writing was bold, impatient, distinctive. The signature was *Ben.* She felt better.

A smile was still lifting the corners of her mouth when, half an hour later, she met Jenny Platt in the cloakroom, endeavouring to smooth down the mop of naturally curly hair that was the bane of her life. What sort of power image could she ever hope to project, looking like the fairy from the top of the Christmas tree?

'Jenny. I've just had a quick look at the statement you got

from Callaghan's girlfriend yesterday. How did you get on with her?'

Jenny pulled a face. 'Some girl! Forty if she's a day.' She hesitated to add that she'd thought Claire Denton a real hard-faced bitch, which was true but might be construed as personal prejudice.

She was saved as Abigail went on, 'I see he was live on TV until ten-thirty, after which she swears he spent the night at her flat. How reliable is she? Would she perjure herself for him?'

'She was at pains to show it was an affair with no strings attached, but I wouldn't put it past her to lie for him, depending on what's in it for her. And from what she said, it looks like it was a last-minute arrangement, so he could've set it up to provide himself with an alibi.'

'Well, thanks, Jenny. As an alibi, it's not what I'd call bomb-proof, but whose is, so far? Not a decent one between the lot of 'em.' Abigail gave her nose a cursory pat with her powder puff. 'After the briefing with the DCI, I'd like you to come out with me to see a woman called Naomi Graham. I have a feeling I'm going to need some moral support.'

'Right, I'll be ready, ma'am.'

Abigail knew things were on their way back to normal the moment she put her nose in the door of the incident room and had to fight her way through the rich fug of George Atkins's pipe smoke. 'Good to see you back again, George. 'Flu gone?'

Officially, that was what the inspector had been off work with – 'flu. The station grapevine said he'd been off to have his bunions seen to. Abigail felt he could be allowed his small touch of vanity: he was a maddening old devil at times, but he was invaluable, with his infinite capacity for tedious, detailed work, his knowledge of the locality and his elephantine memory for villains and all their works. He relit his pipe and said in answer to her question, 'Fit as I'll ever be until I leave this madhouse permanently behind, thanks.' George, according to himself, couldn't wait for his retirement. There were those who believed otherwise, predicted he'd last six months, if that, without the prop of Milford Road nick. Still more who believed that it might be Milford Road which would collapse without George Atkins. Observing the back-log of documents which he'd relieved her of and was now steadily working through, Abigail was inclined to come down on the side of the angels. She thanked heaven and went to the table at the front of the room, ready for the essential daily exchange of information and ideas.

'If we're talking about motives,' Carmody pointed out, after all the usual routine of comment, report and observation had been gone through, and most of the team had dispersed to their various allocated duties, 'we shouldn't forget Matthew Wilding. He's nineteen years old, not getting on too well with his old man, not exactly enthusiastic about selling jewel-lery as a career and rarin' to be off rally driving. The only thing he was short of before was money. And now, bingo!'

Jenny arrived with cups of coffee made from the special supply she kept for the favoured few first thing in the morn-ing, and Abigail perched on the edge of the desk, cradling the mug, sipping the hot liquid, black and strong – the only decent cup she was likely to get that day. She'd been through all this and more, over and over again at various sleepless points during the night and got nowhere.

'Carry on, Ted.' Mayo was interested. It was always worth listening to what Carmody had to say. With his dry native Liverpudlian common sense, if he wasn't always right on the mark, he was usually near.

Mayo was sitting in on the briefing as usual, reinforcing Abigail's jaded feeling by his quick grasp of every detail. How the devil did he manage to keep *au fait* with so many cases, juggle so many balls in the air at once? It was a trick – an art – she was trying very hard to learn, and discovering that it didn't come easy. Whereas Mayo would no doubt go away, put on somebody's seventh symphony and have it all worked out by the time it was finished. It never worked like that for Abigail.

She braced herself to go through yet another rehash of the facts, telling herself there was always the chance of finding some new, unthought-of angle, of coming across some small but significant fact that had somehow been missed.

Carmody's face bore its usual doleful expression, his brow furrowed like a perplexed basset hound's as he continued. 'If he knew money was coming to him when Nigel died and decided he couldn't wait, he had everything going for him. He knew Nigel would be working late, he had keys, he'd have no problem getting hold of one of his dad's trucks to get the body out of the way –'

'He was also dead drunk,' Abigail reminded him.

'So he was,' Carmody said. '*And* he knew about that missing box being in the safe.'

Abigail had already made a mental note that it was time she had another go at old George Fontenoy about the box – and that she wouldn't let him get away without an answer this time. Wasn't it stretching it a bit to believe that he really hadn't known what was in it? Would he have been so cagey all along about it if he hadn't suspected it had played an important part in the murder?

'We'd better have young Wilding in then,' Mayo said, 'and see what he's got to say for himself. Lean on him a bit, but not like a ton of bricks. His father has connections with too many people with clout in this town to upset him. Kid gloves treatment needed on this one. Without, of course,' he added, 'diluting our efforts.'

He smiled blandly and, having finished his coffee, went out.

He's already thinking like a super, thought Abigail, watching him leave the office. She said to Carmody, still feeling mildly bitchy, 'What time does he clock on, for God's sake? I was here at the crack of dawn but he'd beaten me to it. I swear if I arrived at half-five he'd have been here since quarter-to.'

After Jenny Platt had driven her out to see Naomi Graham and they had received no reply to their repeated knockings, Abigail returned and settled down to a hard morning's work, rereading witness statements, sifting through the information amassed so far, and in between ringing Naomi

Graham several times but getting no answer. By lunchtime, the early morning euphoria engendered by Ben's postcard had lessened even more. With an increasingly frustrated feeling that something, somewhere, was lacking, some fact which either hadn't yet emerged, or had been missed, she went out to lunch with Carmody.

19

If a postcard from Ben couldn't permanently lift Abigail's mild depression, then lunch at the Triangle Café had no chance. Abigail found herself turning to the view from the window, boringly familiar but offering some diversion from the greasy egg, sausages and chips in front of her, a meal which should have come with a suicide warning.

'Not hungry?' Carmody asked as she laid down her knife and fork.

'I've suddenly lost my appetite.' She pushed her plate away and peered through the steam within and the rain streaming down the windows outside, in order to try to get a better view of Next on the opposite side of the road. There was a suit she thought she might fancy in the window, but every time she craned her neck to get a better look her attempt was foiled by a passing bus or lorry, their wheels throwing up curtains of spray from the wet tarmac, or by some woman under a large umbrella stopping in front of the window.

'Better bet than the salads.' This was indisputable. There they sat, ready prepared and limp on the counter, a lettuce leaf with tomato and cucumber, with the exciting alternatives of either a hard-boiled egg smothered in salad cream, an unlikely-shaped rectangle of ham or a pile of grated kitchen soap masquerading as cheese.

He laughed at the expression on her face. 'Never mind, I'll stand you a doughnut to have with your tea.'

Abigail smiled and felt better. Carmody had that effect on her. Saddled with an appearance that made him look depressed even when he wasn't, he was tough and experienced and never let things get him down. Probably he'd sensed her impatience and frustration, how conscious she was that her reputation was on the line, knowing that a lot depended on how she showed up in this investigation and knowing how easily she could come a cropper. Carmody himself never worried about things like that, but she was grateful for his unflappable support. They hadn't worked together for very long but, outwardly an unlikely pair, their skills and strengths were beginning to dovetail together, like two halves of a broken sixpence. Something in the thought made her pause, her mind blipped, a sudden light pierced the darkness like a peak pulse on a radar screen, then the image was gone.

Their table was by the window, overlooking the high street and part of the market. Rain gurgled in the gutters, dripped off the brightly coloured canopies of the market stalls and the noses of pedestrians. The streets of market day Lavenstock, however, were as thronged with shoppers as they always were, seemingly unaffected by the weather.

'That looks like Matthew Wilding over there,' she remarked to Carmody, who had polished off both his sausages and was eyeing hers.

It *was* Matthew, hunched into an anorak but bare-headed, his short, crisp hair slick with rain. He was with another, bigger and fairer young man. Shouldering their way through the crowds, they were moving along at a smart clip, absorbed in conversation, heedless of puddles and cutting across the road on the red light, seconds after it had changed from amber, pursued by horn-blasts from several enraged drivers.

'It's our Matthew, though it won't be much longer if that's the way he carries on,' answered Carmody, observing this. 'You going to eat that sausage?'

'Have it with pleasure. If you dare.'

'You wouldn't be so picky if you were married to Maureen. Wonderful woman, but not much in the cordon bleu stakes,' Carmody admitted, spearing the sausage on the end of his fork and spreading it liberally with mustard as Matthew and his companion came to a halt in front of Halfords.

'That young man seems to have made a remarkable recovery from the shock and horror of last night's revelation,'

Abigail said. 'And he must have a more forgiving nature than I'd have given him credit for, if that's who I think it is with him . . . Naomi Graham's son, what's-his-name?' She didn't know why she was so sure of the other person's identity, but she was, watching the two of them gazing at motor spares, lubricating oil and cans of touch-up paint with all the absorption of children with their noses pressed to a toy shop window.

'Joss. That's him all right.' Carmody had total recall for names and he'd met Joss during the questioning of the men on Jake Wilding's building site. 'Matthew's half-brother, if everybody is to be believed.'

'Yes,' Abigail said, thinking of course, the family resemblance again. 'He's the one who gave Matthew his alibi, right? The one he goes rally driving with. The one who happened to get a job with Jake Wilding. Now there's a cluster of coincidences, if you like.'

'I don't believe in coincidences,' Carmody said, with all the unshakeable conviction of a flat-earther.

'Neither do I, Ted. Come on.'

'No pud?'

Abigail's look said what she thought of any pudding likely to be served at the Triangle. They'd only come here because it was market day and every other place was full, and because the food was said to be better than the canteen food, which was a lie.

But by the time they'd paid up and extricated their macs and made their way outside, ready to cross to Halfords, something about the pair had altered Abigail's perceptions, and she tugged at Carmody's sleeve. 'Wait a minute, Ted.' The two were still gazing into the window, but it was patently obvious from the angry profiles occasionally turned to each other that they were in the middle of a blazing row. Even as Abigail noted this, Matthew, with a black look at his companion, strode off, splashing with furious abandon through the puddles. The other turned and watched him go with narrowed eyes, then, shrugging his shoulders, made rapid headway in the other direction.

'It's time I had a word with Joss Graham,' Abigail announced.

Carmody, looking enigmatic, said she was in for a treat.

Mayo had made his last appearance in court on this particular case. The judge's summing up had been mercifully brief, and the jury had come out after only two hours, giving the guilty verdict the prosecution had been hoping for. He was feeling benevolent. The rain had stopped and the sun made the air glitter like April. And he grinned like a Cheshire cat every time he thought about the letter from Alex which had come that morning.

He'd arranged to see DI Moon in his office and while he waited, asked for a tray of tea to be sent up and went to inspect the clock he'd placed on top of the filing cabinet, now looking nothing like the clapped-out old wreck he'd found on a market stall. He was pleased with the results of his labours, all the hours of his spare time spent in polishing the slate case and cleaning up the brass spandrels and, with infinite patience, repairing, cleaning and oiling the works. It could now be seen as the handsome Victorian marble mantel clock it was, nothing very exciting, but a respectable addition to his collection of venerable timepieces. Its tick was comfortable, it had a sweet chime. It still wasn't keeping perfect time, so he'd brought it into the office where he could keep an eye on it. He regulated it now, checking the correct time with his watch, and went back to the bulky file, open on his desk. If only human beings were as easily adjustable!

'I've been having another look at the file,' he said when Abigail was settled before him with a cup of tea. 'We know Matthew Wilding was out with Joss Graham last Friday night and got himself plastered, right? Have we checked where they did their drinking, yet?'

'Farrar did. He's just reported back and – you're going to love this, sir – it was the Rose.'

'What?'

Mayo's mind immediately charted new possibilities, though Abigail's next words quickly stemmed the flow of speculation. 'Farrar says that Sal Cellini confirms they were there until about half past ten and that young Matthew was apparently stoned out of his head. They weren't exactly thrown out, but they would have been if Graham hadn't responded to the suggestion that they leave, PDQ. He thinks Cellini might know more than he's saying about that.'

'Stoned on something more than alcohol, is that what he means?'

'Possibly, but if he suspects it, he isn't saying.'

'Then if Matthew was that far out of his head, from whatever cause, it makes it doubtful that he could have murdered and disposed of Fontenoy in the way he was.'

'And Lindsay Hammond confirmed that he got home about eleven, anyway. She was wakened by car headlights, or that's what she says.'

'No obvious reason why she should be lying, is there?'

'No-o. Nothing I can put a finger on. I just have a funny feeling about her.' Abigail frowned, then made a dismissive gesture and went on to tell him of the apparent quarrel she'd witnessed between Matthew Wilding and Joss Graham. 'I've been trying to get hold of Naomi Graham since first thing this morning. I called at the house and I've been telephoning every hour since, but no joy. So I thought I'd go and see Joss Graham at the building site.'

'What are we waiting for?' Mayo reached for his jacket. 'If we go now, we'll catch them before the light goes and they have to knock off.'

'Where did you find it?' asked Christine. She recognized the ring instantly and felt a plunging sensation in the pit of her stomach.

'Under the corner of the rug in Lindsay's room.'

Mrs Knight's tone could not have been described as anything other than accusing, as if Christine, like some Victorian mistress, had put the ring there purposely, to test whether she'd lifted the rug to clean under it or not. In actual fact, Mrs Knight's thoroughness was the one thing Christine couldn't complain about. She even rolled out the cooker in the kitchen to clean behind it. But she was an unappealing woman who went about her twice-weekly cleaning with a self-righteous ferocity, as if defying anyone to imply she resented performing such menial tasks. She was the comfortably-off wife of one of the local Labour councillors and only did the job to prove that all women were equal.

She held the ring out as if it were something unspeakable. Her bright hard eyes stared at Christine. 'Looks valuable to me.' The subtext being: *Some people have more money than sense, not taking care of what they have.* 'I thought I'd better give it you rather than just putting it on the dressing table.' Subtext: *So if there's any question about it, I'm in the clear.*

Christine, who had previously always worked on the principle that if you had anyone working in the house, it had to be someone you could get on with, suddenly asked herself why she was putting up with someone she disliked so much. She decided that was it. She would find a suitable time, and tell Mrs Knight that she could go.

She busied herself now with other things until the lady had departed in her smugly elderly Mini and she and Lindsay were alone in the house after lunch. They were in the sitting room, Lindsay sitting cross-legged on the floor in front of the huge window that overlooked the garden, cradling her lute. She had been playing a plaintive Renaissance song, singing softly to it in her sweet alto, and the echoes still hung in the room. Christine was loath to break the mood, she couldn't recall the last time she'd heard Lindsay playing or singing. Until her illness, she'd been a star pupil, full of promise – and soon would be again, of course, now that she was getting better. Christine took a deep breath and dropped the ring on the coffee table, telling Lindsay where it had been found.

Lindsay immediately looked panic-stricken, her face flushing a dull and unbecoming red. 'It must have slipped off my finger.'

'That's not surprising – it must be several sizes too big for you. It's a man's ring.'

With infinite care, Lindsay put her lute down on the carpet next to her. 'I had it on my thumb,' she said, inexplicably.

Christine's face mirrored Lindsay's dismay as they both looked down at the Janus ring, sitting balefully on the polished walnut, light refracted from the glowing, deep blue stone.

'You've never shown me this before. Where did you get it?'

Lindsay looked quickly at her mother and saw that Christine had recognized the ring as being the one which Fontenoy's had had in stock for quite some time, one which Nigel had on occasion worn. She thought rapidly, then took a deep breath and told her that Nigel had given it to her, weeks ago. Christine picked it up again and clenched it in her fist. 'You never used to lie to me, Lindsay.'

'I'm not lying now.'

But Christine knew that she was. And that Lindsay knew that she knew. The full implication of what this might mean hit Christine and, as if the realization had caused scales to fall from her eyes, she suddenly saw a great deal more than she had hitherto about Lindsay's condition over the last few months. A lot of puzzling questions were answered. Glandular fever? What a fool she'd been!

The painful knowledge came to her that she'd failed her daughter. Otherwise, why had Lindsay not felt able to confide in her, ask for her help? Quickly following on came the realization, however, that a mother might well be the last person any girl would tell in the circumstances – especially one who was preoccupied with reshaping her own life, remarrying, happier than she had been for years – but I honestly didn't think I was that sort of mother, Christine thought desolately.

But *who* had been responsible for doing this to her daughter? And with another shock, a name immediately came to her. In her mind's eye she saw Lindsay talking to him at the wedding reception, eyes full of tears, drinking champagne and looking as though she wished it were hemlock.

'If someone else hadn't already killed him, I'd do it myself,' she said through her teeth.

'Mum?'

'Just tell me the truth, Lindsay – about everything. Don't be afraid I won't understand. You're not the first to have had this happen. It was an abortion you had, wasn't it?'

The Janus ring bit into her palm. The two-faced god, which couldn't be more appropriate. Lindsay went red again, then white. She stood up abruptly. I mustn't fail her again, I must think what to do for the best, thought Christine, as she went to take Lindsay in her arms, only to have her back away, her eyes wide.

'You think – you think – *Nigel*? Oh, but that's *gross*!'

Although immediately realizing the enormity of her mistake, Christine noticed that Lindsay didn't deny the abortion itself. 'It wasn't Nigel? Who was it, then?'

For a long time, Lindsay said nothing. 'Nobody who matters,' she said at last, in a low voice. 'A boy I knew at school. After a party. You won't believe it, but it was the first time.'

'Of course I would, if you say so.' And, knowing Lindsay, she might be so consumed with guilt that Christine could well believe it might be the last. She needed help. At the same time, she knew that Lindsay wasn't ready for that, she wouldn't talk to her yet, she'd need time before she could. She'd only clam up if she were pressed now.

'Well, Lindsay, what about this ring? How did you come by it?'

'I can't tell you that, I can't!'

This is murder we're talking about, Christine said to herself, it's no time for being squeamish, or soft, even if you suspect your child of unimaginable horrors. Her resolve strengthened. She made herself sound firmer than she felt.

'What are you going to do?' Lindsay asked nervously.

'It's not up to me, Lindsay, it's what you have to do, isn't it?'

20

The narrow road, a turning off the main road, wound upwards into the partially developed housing site. A large board at the entrance announced:

FORDE MANOR GARDENS

ANOTHER PRESTIGIOUS DEVELOPMENT

BY

WILDING HOMES.

LUXURY THREE-BEDROOM AND FOUR-BEDROOM HOUSES.
PHASE ONE NEARING COMPLETION.

Home and Dry with Wilding Homes!

The site was imaginatively designed. Several small cul-de-sacs and crescents led off the central main road which wound sinuously up the hill, some of the front gardens already partly landscaped.

Ask for Thelma, they'd been told, and were now directed to the site office, housed in a portakabin near the bottom of the site, down among the earth-moving equipment and the wire-meshed compound where raw materials and machinery stood.

Considering the state of the unmade roads and the rain of the previous day, which had left behind a sea of red mud, the office was unbelievably spick and span, smelling strongly of floral air-freshener. At an equally sterile desk sat Thelma, papers neatly spread and a small computer switched on as an indication that she'd been working on them. A Mills & Boon paperback peeped out from under a file.

'Oh, it's you again!' she said when she knew they were the police. 'When are you going to let us have that pick-up back? Mr Wilding's going spare.' She was a redoubtable-looking woman, with a middle-aged perm and too much make-up, sucking a sweet. Despite the unenthusiastic greeting, their arrival had obviously created a welcome diversion and when the coolness had worn off, she was ready to help. The police activity and subsequent inquiries which had already taken place on the site, the questioning of the first-aider about any recent on-site accident involving quantities of blood, must have had the place jumping with speculation and she was no doubt hopeful of picking up some tasty titbit of gossip.

'Joss Graham?' Transferring the sweet from one cheek to the other, she informed them that today they'd find him working on one of the houses near the entrance to the site. They must already have passed him. He had no specific duties but worked at whatever job he was told to do. 'And very willingly,' she added approvingly. 'Joss never minds what he does. Not like some. But being so much better educated, he's no need to stand on his dignity, has he? You know he's a microbiologist?'

'Is that so?' Mayo felt obliged to show the surprise Thelma evidently expected. 'What's he doing working here, then?'

'He couldn't get a job in his own field, but he's not the sort to be too proud to take what he can get.' Clearly, Thelma saw herself as cheerleader of the Joss Graham fan club. Mayo thanked her, prepared to meet a cross between Einstein and the Archangel Gabriel.

'Go up Lineker Road and then Christie Avenue, and you'll find him at the first house in Mansell Crescent,' Thelma had said. Before going up there, however, Mayo decided to take a look at the collapsed ruin of the old house, Forde Manor, less than a hundred yards away. The vehicle tracks Carmody had mentioned had been obscured by the recent heavy rain, but the flattened fence hadn't yet been repaired, leaving a clear view of the field beyond. It told them nothing. There was nothing to see, apart from a heap of rubble. Incredibly, scarcely one brick had been left standing on another and it was impossible to tell what the original house had been like. They left the desolate scene behind and went in search of Joss Graham.

He was working on what was to be the front garden of one of the houses, sitting on a yellow-painted excavator and manipulating it to cut out the curving driveway as delicately and precisely as if with a knife and fork, manoeuvring round the porcelain bathroom fixtures which stood waiting outside the front door to be carried in.

Abigail wondered if she could have met him before and then decided that it was the glimpse she'd had of him yesterday that had made her think so. He was a type, there was at least one on every building site, a big, macho bloke with a tanned, outdoor complexion. Under a yellow hard hat, longish, wavy fair hair that any girl would have been proud of. Very blue eyes, one earring and a lazy smile. He leaned out of the cab to speak, looking down on them. The smile was directed at Abigail, not Mayo, whom he largely ignored. He was the sort to have been stripped to the waist, had it not been so cold. As it was, he wore nothing more than jeans and a check work shirt, pushed up to the elbows so that the tattoos on his forearm were only partly covered.

He had stopped work, switching the machine to idle as they approached. Mayo showed his warrant card and told him they were making further investigations into the murder of Nigel Fontenoy.

'The guy who had the antique shop, yeah. Yeah, I know. I've heard Matt Wilding talk about him.'

'Ever met him?'

'You think I move in those sort of circles?'

'Is there somewhere we can talk?' Mayo asked, giving him a sharp look.

'Sure.' Graham switched the machine off, jumped down and led them into the kitchen of the house next door to the one with the bathroom fittings outside. There was a smell of damp plaster and new wood. The kitchen was finished, and there was an electric kettle, coffee mugs, a jar of instant coffee and a bag of sugar on the counter. 'Like a coffee?'

Mayo waved the suggestion away. 'Thanks, but we don't want to keep you from your work. Inspector Moon here has one or two more questions to ask you. It shouldn't take long.' Graham had, like the rest of the workforce, previously been questioned, but now that his connections with both Jake and Matthew Wilding were known, it was necessary to be more specific.

'Feel free.' He had a pleasant voice and a classless intonation, but his conversation was sprinkled with too many of these deliberate Americanisms, which Mayo found irritating. He nodded to Abigail and leaned back against the sink, while Graham hitched himself on to a corner of the central unit.

It didn't take Abigail long to establish that Joss Graham was no product of the higher education system of this country, or any other. His schooling had stopped when he was fifteen, legally or illegally hardly mattered now. The job he was doing here was similar to the dozens of other unskilled jobs he'd worked at around the world. What would Thelma say when that piece of news percolated through to her? Mayo decided she'd find some excuse to justify it. Like a few bits of paper saying what exams you'd passed not equating with intelligence, or some such. Possibly true, in Joss Graham's case. He was obviously no fool.

'Why did you lie to Mr Wilding about your qualifications?' Abigail was asking.

'I wanted the job. I wasn't the only one going for it and I figured if there was any choice, it would give me a head start.' His lips twisted in a smile little short of insolence. 'Mr Wilding, having none himself, is impressed by that sort of thing.'

'Mr Wilding took you on himself? Doesn't he leave that to his foreman, or personnel manager or whatever?'

'Mr Wilding never allows *anyone* to work for him without his say so.'

'Wouldn't it have been easier simply to tell him who you were? That he was your father?' Mayo put in.

'Who says he's my father?' A brief, blazing look came from the blue eyes, but was quickly extinguished.

'Your mother seems to think he is.'

'Well, she should know.' With a lazy grin, Graham tipped his yellow hat further over his brow, folding his arms. 'But you shouldn't really believe everything my mother says.'

'We're not playing games here, Graham!' Mayo intervened sharply. 'A man's been murdered, in case you've forgotten.'

'Right. But what has that to do with me, or my parentage?'

'For your sake nothing, I hope. For the moment, I'd like to know just what your game is – why you came here to work at all?'

'Isn't a guy entitled to be curious about someone who might be his father? If I liked what I saw, who knows? If I didn't, I could always forget it.'

So far, he hadn't given a single straightforward answer, and Mayo felt he was wasting his time hoping to get one, on this subject at any rate. But he knew he'd get nowhere losing his temper with Graham, and there were other questions to ask. 'We'll come back to that later, Graham. Meanwhile, let's see if you can do any better at telling us where you were the night Nigel Fontenoy died, and I don't want any funny answers.'

Graham was unfazed. 'Your people have already been through all this.'

'Never mind that, it won't do any harm to go over it again.'

'OK, OK, go ahead.'

Was he naturally so laid back – or was it a put-on, designed to hide deeper feelings? Mayo thought not. Something told him that what you saw was what you got, as far as Joss Graham was concerned. And he didn't particularly like what he saw; there was that underlying arrogance that set his teeth on edge for one thing – plus a feeling that Graham was laughing up his sleeve, as if he knew something they didn't know, which did nothing to endear him to Mayo.

'You and Matthew Wilding were out drinking the night Nigel Fontenoy was murdered,' he said. 'I suppose you can remember that far back?'

'Sure I remember. It's a night Matt won't forget in a hurry, either. First time he was ever drunk – and I mean drunk! He was knocking them back like there was no tomorrow.'

'What about you?'

'Me? Oh, I've learned how to hold my drink.'

That wasn't what Sal Cellini had originally said. Later, he'd admitted that he'd had a suspicion that Graham wasn't as drunk as he appeared, but had been egging the younger man on unnecessarily. The question of drugs had crossed the nightclub owner's mind, but he'd decided they were only boozed up. All the same, he'd asked them to leave – he'd had a suspicion the lad might not have been as old as he said he was.

'Didn't you try and stop Matthew?' Abigail put in.

'No, why should I? It's an experience everybody has to go through sometime, it's part of growing up.'

'That's one point of view.'

'Oh, come on, he's *nineteen*! And I guess he was entitled to kick over the traces that night.'

'Why that night, in particular?'

'Just a feeling I had, maybe he'd had a row with his father, I don't know. He's all mixed up about his relations with him, doesn't really like being as rebellious as he makes out he is.'

'So – Matthew got completely drunk – then what?'

'I drove him home. I was hesitating about leaving him alone, but as soon as he got out of the car, he threw up. I knew he'd be OK after that, all he needed was to sleep it off. He was making one hell of a racket, though, and Lindsay came out to see what was going on. She said to leave him to her, she'd make him some coffee, get him to bed, so that's what I did.'

'What time was that?'

'Around eleven, eleven-fifteen maybe. I don't keep much track of time.'

'Where did you go from there?'

'Home, of course.'

'And got there at what time?'

'Must've been around eleven-forty-five, or a bit earlier.'

'Jake Wilding was still there?'

'*Jake*? You're not serious?'

'He says he was visiting your mother.'

Amusement lifted the corner of Graham's mouth. 'Was he? Well, if he says so. Maybe he parked his car around the corner. Sure, there was a light in the front room, but my mother often stays up late. I went in the back way and straight upstairs so as not to disturb her.'

'So she couldn't confirm what time you got in?'

'No, but my sister Cassie would. I knocked on her door as I went past. Thought the storm might be bothering her. She asked me what time it was and I said coming up to midnight.'

In that case, he couldn't have been murdering Nigel Fontenoy in the middle of Lavenstock. But . . . *another* sister, half-sister, whatever, providing *another* alibi? All these sibling permutations could give you a headache.

The sun was emerging from behind the clouds as they left the site, one of those brilliant shafts on a dark afternoon that light a scene with a lurid unreality. Joss Graham was standing beside the JCB, watching them, waiting to climb back into the seat, and some trick of that odd light made his profile stand out for one brief, illuminating moment in sharp relief. In that moment, Abigail was again aware of that eerie feeling of recognition. Her pulses quickening, she knew that what she'd just seen, and something else she had previously noticed and recorded in her subconscious, had slotted together. She felt a faint chill down her spine but her intuition refused to take her any further.

She took the wheel and, as they left the site, Mayo remarked, 'I think we could be on to something here, Abigail. He's lying in his teeth. What's he being so damned cagey about, if he hasn't something to hide – all that guff about Wilding, implying he isn't his father! You've only got to look at him to see the likeness.'

'You reckon, sir?'

'Why, don't you?'

'It's possible –'

'And so are a lot more things. Like Graham having easy access to Wilding's truck, like him being a big strong lad, physically capable of manhandling Fontenoy's body, like having an alibi that stinks. He'd ample opportunity after leaving Matthew Wilding, and only his sister to say what time he got in. But what about the motive? Why should he want to murder Fontenoy? If it had been *Wilding* who was

164

murdered, now – well, it's pretty obvious he hates Jake Wilding's guts . . .'

Abigail said, 'He and Matthew Wilding have alibied each other. What if they were in it together?'

'The same thought had crossed my mind. Matthew stood to gain a lot from Fontenoy's death, and could've made it worth Graham's while to help him. But you know, I'm still bothered by that missing box. We must assume that *was* the parcel Fontenoy took up to London – and unless he left it there, it went missing from the safe on the night he was killed, so it's therefore crucial to the murder. I'm looking for something which would explain that. Such as Fontenoy sending the box to Naomi Graham via Wilding, in exchange for that document she's alleged to have.'

The phrase she had used about herself and Carmody, and which had been inexplicably haunting her ever since, suddenly came back to Abigail in a different context. Two halves of a sixpence. The broken coin, the lovers' token, the conspirators' map torn in two, both halves of which must dovetail . . . it seemed like a notion straight out of romantic adventure fiction, *Boys' Own Paper* stuff. And yet . . .

'I may be way out on this, sir,' she said slowly, 'but supposing it wasn't an *exchange* Fontenoy had in mind. What if those two belonged together – the document of Naomi Graham's, and the contents of Nigel Fontenoy's box – that neither was complete without the other . . .'

Mayo's interest was caught. 'Go on.'

'If we assume Fontenoy *did* take the box to Jermyn's, it seems reasonable to think it contained – well, certainly not papers, as Christine Wilding suggested, but the sort of thing Jermyn's would be interested in – jewellery of some kind.'

'That's feasible.' Warming to the idea, Mayo added, 'And Naomi's document could be the provenance for it, the proof of its authenticity. The thing that would up the ante many times. Good thinking, Abigail. And supposing Wilding knew about the box – through Christine – and he now has both, hm? When shall we be able to talk to Jermyn's man?'

'He gets back tomorrow. But if he doesn't know anything about what was in the box, I don't really see how we can find out, other than putting the thumbscrews on old George Fontenoy.'

'Well, we're making a lot of assumptions anyway which may be unjustified. The thing to do is to get hold of Naomi Graham – and as soon as possible.'

Abigail looked at him quickly. 'Yes, Nigel Fontenoy may have been killed for the contents of that box. And if Naomi Graham still has the document . . .'

'Well, I don't like the way this is pointing, but let's not get ahead of ourselves. Let's see we keep tabs on our friend back there on the building site. Meanwhile, if we haven't already had Wilding junior in yet, I think I'll see him myself.'

Abigail, as she drove back to the station, was again tantalized by that last glimpse of Joss Graham, aware that some sort of connective idea was forming in the back of her mind. What if –? she thought suddenly. No, she was jumping the gun, guessing. But what if her guess, hunch, intuition, call it what you will, was right?

She didn't mention what she'd just thought to Mayo, not yet, not until she had seen Naomi Graham and could be more sure. Mayo didn't go much on hunches and she'd already come up with one about the box and its provenance which might be way out. She wasn't going to push her luck.

21

Naomi Graham had spent most of the day feverishly clearing out, preparatory to packing, answering neither the door nor the telephone, hoping to finish before Cassie got home. It was hopeless, even with the assistance of a glass or two of wine. It remained a total mystery to her how she, surely the most unacquisitive person alive, had managed to amass so many possessions, and was only to be explained by the fact that her stay in Lavenstock had lasted far longer than she'd originally meant it to. Things had simply accumulated, mostly as a result of living in this terrible climate. So much more was needed, not only in the way of clothes against the cold and the wet, but blankets, heaters, hot water bottles, things unnecessary and unimagined in the Mediterranean countries that were fast acquiring in Naomi's mind all the attractions of the Isles of the Blest.

Cassie, arriving home long before Naomi had finished and finding her mother with a glass in her hand, contemplating with despair the chaos she had created, stared accusingly at her across the mess like some goddess of vengeance, her dark face flushed, her black luxuriant hair vibrant and electric, her dark eyes flashing, all Greek.

'What are you doing?' she demanded.

'Isn't it obvious? I'm getting ready to leave. I've had enough of this place!' Naomi declared, waving her glass.

An InterCity express, on the up-line to Birmingham, made its presence felt, shaking the window-frames until the panes rattled, while Cassie watched her mother with narrowed eyes. When she could make herself clearly heard, she declared, her mouth passionate, 'I won't go with you.'

'I never imagined you would,' Naomi replied, with undisguised relief. For a moment there, she had imagined Cassie was going to suggest accompanying her.

Cassie regarded her mother with pitying scorn. She herself had not, it was true, ever made any secret of her wish to remain in England. She'd no desire to begin the penniless, vagabond life with her mother all over again. She was determined, in fact, that nothing would make her. But behind the wariness at the back of her mind, the panic, even, behind the questions as to why her mother was really leaving, was the feeling that it would have been nice to have been asked.

'You can stay on here, until the house is sold,' Naomi offered, feeling she was being more than generous. Mundane considerations such as how Cassie was to keep it going on her part-time wages from the filling station or what would happen to her when it was eventually sold, hadn't entered her head – or if they had, she'd assumed Cassie would manage somehow, as Naomi herself always had. As she had now, for instance, having managed to winkle out someone to stay with in Turkey, until the house was sold. Cassie was young, she had a fierce energy and self-reliance and besides, Naomi had a duty to herself, hadn't she? But whether the house was sold or not was ultimately of little account, money was the last thing that mattered to her. All that counted now was to shake the dust of Lavenstock from her heels forever. It was imperative to move on.

She had no regrets. Nothing good had ever happened here, everything bad. Worse would happen if she stayed. Things had changed with Nigel's death. She shivered as though someone had walked over her own grave. For a moment, her thoughts were insupportable but, as always, she shrugged them off. Only two things remained to be done: to write a letter, and to see George Fontenoy. It was nigh on twenty years since she'd last seen old George, but she didn't expect him to have changed. Unlike Nigel, he'd always been an eminently reasonable man and, in a nicer way than Nigel with his pretty little girlies, had had a soft spot for a handsome young woman, she recalled, forgetting that she was no longer either handsome, or young.

She came out of her thoughts to see Cassie shrugging herself back into her leather jacket, a sullen, determined look on her face. It was the sort of look that Naomi had come to dread, the look that Cassie and Joss shared.

'Where are you going?'

'To see Joss, amongst other things. Don't worry,' Cassie added, which was a mere figure of speech because she knew her mother was incapable of it, 'I'll be back.'

In a few moments, her motorbike could be heard roaring away. Naomi shut her eyes for a moment against an unfamiliar, choking despair, then poured herself more wine.

Having knocked several times on the front door of the ramshackle little house above the railway cutting and received no reply, Jenny Platt was about to go round to the back when the door was suddenly opened by a woman who stared at them without speaking.

Abigail introduced herself and Jenny, and explained why they were there. 'I take it you've no objection to answering a few questions, Mrs Graham?'

'I was never Mrs Graham, Mrs Andreas either, but it'll do if you want to be formal. I prefer Naomi. Come in.'

Jenny raised a quizzical eyebrow in Abigail's direction as they were shown without haste into a small front parlour that had a musty, unused feeling and yet at the same time spoke eloquently of too many people living in too little space. Every surface was cluttered, including the floor. The tacky furniture, apart from a large TV set and some seriously expensive sound equipment, had the appearance of having come from the nearest Oxfam shop, which was in fact the case. The tall, untidy woman who had shown them in was dressed in a random assortment of clothes, apparently from the same source as the furniture. Her feet were bare and a little grubby, a silky shawl with a matted fringe slipped from her shoulders. She was a 1960s fugitive, yet, beneath the tat and the undisciplined grey hair, the slackness round her jaw, it was possible to see that she might once have been very attractive.

Seats were found for them by adding more to the piles of everything else on the floor. 'Drink?' Naomi asked, waving the bottle, and when the offer had politely been declined, topped up her own glass. This done, she subsided on to the carpet, sitting in the lotus position with the wine bottle handy and answering Abigail's questions, if not willingly, at least truthfully, as far as Abigail could tell. Yes, Jake Wilding was her first husband. Yes, he had visited her on the night of Nigel Fontenoy's death. Yes, the inspector had the times of his visit substantially correct. And *no*, she had not handed over to him a letter or document, or anything to give to Nigel Fontenoy, she couldn't imagine what Nigel could possibly have been on about. Her voice was suddenly sharp-edged with malice, a secretive expression crossed her face.

'Are you sure about that, Mrs Graham?'

'Why should I lie?' Why indeed, especially so obviously?

'What was it Nigel Fontenoy so desperately wanted from you?'

'Oh, please! I've told you, I gave him nothing. Even though he sent Jake to persuade me rather than face me himself. And offered me *money*.' She said this as though it was the ultimate insult. 'Nigel always did think money was the answer to everything.'

Abigail said suddenly, 'Why do you think he was murdered?'

'Why are you asking me that?' she demanded, suddenly stiff-lipped. 'What makes you think I'd know?'

'Because, Mrs Graham – Naomi – we think it might be because of something he had in his possession. If you *do* have this document, has it occurred to you that *you* might be in danger?'

This seemed to frighten her more but her mouth stayed stubbornly set. Abigail sighed. 'All right, let's talk about something else. I believe you once worked for Nigel Fontenoy and his father, as a jewellery designer?'

The alacrity with which the other woman answered showed how she welcomed the change of subject. 'Yes, but that was before I left Lavenstock for the first time. I'm leaving again, this time for good. I don't fit in here, I never did.' Her eyes strayed towards a nearly full trunk with its lid propped open, which might partly, but not wholly, have explained the room's untidiness, the recent signs of feverish activity.

Why had she decided to leave Lavenstock now, at this particular juncture? 'You've had a buyer for your house, then?'

'A buyer? Scarcely anybody's even been to view it.' Naomi laughed shortly, unaware that Cassie, showing at least two sets of buyers around in her absence, had skilfully managed to point out the many defects not apparent among the equally numerous and all too obvious ones. 'My mother managed to live happily here for thirty odd years but nobody seems to want anywhere without two bathrooms and central heating nowadays.'

'That's the way it goes.' Abigail smiled sympathetically, but she knew better than to let herself be deflected by discussions of that sort. 'To go back to your jewellery designing –'

The rest was drowned by a noise like the roar of Niagara suddenly filling the room, as two trains rushed past each other through the cutting below. The windows rattled and a small scatter of rubble, dislodged from the chimney, fell down the back of the gas fire to join the dust and the fag-ends and spent matches thrown into the hearth as if it were a real fire.

'It's always like this. You get used to it.' The remark was intended, presumably, to apply to the noise, though it could equally have applied to the general ambience, Abigail was sure. Naomi seemed to be the sort of person whose natural habitat was chaos and confusion.

Doggedly, she went back to her original point. 'What made you give up such interesting work?'

'Perhaps I discovered I'd no talent, after all.'

'That's not what I've heard.'

'My mother has a silver ring you made,' Jenny offered, a fact which had emerged during her conversation with Abigail on the way. 'It's really lovely.'

'Perhaps I came to despise such a decadent trade, then. It doesn't add a lot to the sum of human existence, does it? It caters for women's vanity, that's about all you can say for it.'

It was possible she genuinely felt this, with her jumble sale clothes and a total absence of any jewellery at all – unless this last was a remnant of her designer's fastidiousness, a scorn of wearing any jewellery that was tawdry, or not genuine.

'But you're right about one thing!' Suddenly, Naomi was flushed and animated. 'I did have talent. Why deny it? Here, let me show you something!'

She might have been more loosened up by the wine than Abigail had thought. It could have been that she still had her own small vanities. Whatever it was, with a sudden access of energy, she began scrabbling in the half-packed trunk, throwing out in all directions the clothes which had been more or less folded and put in it, and finally came up with a roughly finished wooden box, inside which was a tray containing tools. Lifting this out, and then using one of the small chisels as a lever, she half prised up the base of the box, which proved to be merely a piece of plywood resting on a fillet of beading, thus forming a shallow cavity, apparently little more than half an inch above the real base. With a slightly furtive gesture, she slid in her hand and extracted a soft suede pouch. Turning it upside down, she allowed a slender gold snake bangle to slide on to her palm. Formed out of strands of differently coloured gold twisted together, the strands knotted halfway, it had a single large garnet glowing at the centre of the knot.

'My apprentice piece.' Naomi's expression was unreadable as she looked at the bangle, which she had slipped on to her forearm, where it wound sinuously downwards with the snake's head resting on her wrist, but she was unable to resist smiling a little when she heard Jenny's drawn-in breath and Abigail's soft exclamation of admiration. 'Derivative, and plenty of mistakes if you know where to look, but not bad, I suppose. I haven't looked at it for years.'

It was hard to associate the free yet disciplined design of the piece and its meticulous execution with this untidy, haphazard woman, the miserably furnished room and what appeared to be a hand to mouth existence. Hard not to make judgements, too, to feel that here was a woman who had wasted her life and talents, and that she must have made many of the difficulties of her life.

Offhanded all at once, wrenching the bangle off, Naomi said, 'Can't think why I've never got rid of it, sold it. It's no use to me and I could've done with the money more times than I can count.'

But Jenny was asking questions about the way it was made, about the different coloured golds, and she couldn't resist explaining. 'Well, you have to add copper to pure gold to make red gold, silver to make green gold and so on.'

'And the engraving?'

'We use these.' Naomi showed them the tools one by one, explaining their traditional uses: pliers, hand clamps, drills, mallets of different kinds, a series of fine needle files with different profiles, punches, a thick, circular mat of closely woven iron wire with a handle which she called a soldering wig, and lastly, sharp chisels called scorpers or burins for engraving, with shaped tips and curious handles, rather like an old-fashioned darning mushroom. She grew animated as she talked, almost as if she'd forgotten they were there. 'It was a good time,' she said wistfully, as she put the tools back, neatly and in order. 'I used to feel like a bird, in those days. Free, able to do anything I wanted.'

Abigail envisaged the sort of girl Naomi might have been – dreamy, impractical, wanting to reach for the stars – but without the will to make it happen. 'What made you leave Lavenstock?' she asked gently.

Naomi upended the wine bottle into her glass and finished it off. Her laugh had a bitter edge. 'I wanted to fly, and he wanted to put me in a cage, simple as that. Marriage is a cage, however you look at it. Especially if you have a child.' She was kneeling on the floor, her head still bent over the trunk. 'God knows why I ever came back, why I ever married Jake. I thought I'd changed, but we don't, do we?'

Abigail was sure now that she had the answer to the question that had been at the back of her mind ever since meeting Joss Graham on the building site. 'But you didn't bring Joss with you when you married Jake, you left him with his grandmother. Why was that?'

A tide of colour suffused Naomi's face, whether through anger or shame or some other emotion it was difficult to tell. 'He was happy where he was, with her – and I was starting a new life. I wanted no encumbrances.'

'Encumbrances? And Jake the child's father –?'

They looked at each other steadily. Naomi seemed just about to speak when into the room came the sudden sound of a motorbike. At which she froze then, galvanized, slammed down the lid of the toolbox, pushed it into the trunk and began throwing the clothes all anyhow on top of the lot. The moment was lost.

A second later the door opened and Abigail found herself looking, somehow without surprise, at the dark, sultry girl she had last seen riding away from the Wilding house.

Cassie came into the room carrying several plastic shopping bags full of groceries, most of them paid for. She nearly always did the shopping. If it had depended on her mother, they wouldn't have eaten at all sometimes, and Cassie was better at providing, anyway. She usually managed to come home with several luxury items they could never legitimately have afforded.

She was not pleased to see two strange women in the house, still less when her mother explained who they were. Naomi was flushed, she looked dangerously bright-eyed in a way only partly explained by the now empty litre bottle of wine. Cassie's heart skipped when she thought of what she might have been saying to the two detectives, and she muttered something about unpacking the shopping and prepared to disappear into the kitchen while she thought of some excuse to get rid of them.

But since there was no reason that Abigail could think of at the moment for detaining Cassie, and since Naomi was now so patently agitated by their presence that it was doubtful if there was any more sense to be got out of her, they left, Abigail maddeningly conscious that the girl's arrival had interrupted the interview just when she had been on the verge of learning something vital.

'If it wasn't too fanciful, I'd almost say she was scared of that girl,' Jenny remarked as they left the house and made their way to the car, which they'd left parked round the corner, out of sight.

The whole of the surrounding area was scheduled for demolition and reconstruction and, desolate though the house was, it was in better shape than the derelict remains of the surrounding railway buildings and a terrace of similar houses, once taken over for motor repair shops and the like, all now abandoned. Abigail shivered.

'Fanciful or not, she frightens me,' she replied, and she was only half joking.

22

While Abigail was finding out what she could from Naomi Graham, Mayo was taking Matthew Wilding through his movements up to, including and after the time of the murder, calmly, slowly, methodically, until there was no minute left unaccounted for. Now, sitting opposite him in an interview room with Carmody beside him and the beefy DC Deeley in attendance, the latter trying without conspicuous success to look unobtrusive, he was taking him through it again, looking for lies or loopholes.

'Let's go back to the Rose,' Mayo said. 'You left at Mr Cellini's request, after being in there drinking since eight o'clock. Joss Graham drove you home, though he wasn't in a fit state, either.'

'If I was so drunk, I wouldn't know about that, would I?' Matthew said hardily.

'Not if you were as drunk as everybody thought you were. But maybe you weren't. Maybe you were just putting on a bit of a show.'

'Why should I do that?'

'To give yourself an alibi, lad. Come to that, why did you get drunk at all that night?'

'I've told you, I don't know. Except that I'd had it in a big way. I was sick of being the meat in the sandwich – my dad being a pain about my rally driving on one side and Nigel on the other.'

'And on top of that, not feeling all that certain now that you want to make a career out of rally driving?'

'I didn't say that. Plenty do. Why shouldn't I?'

Mayo understood what Matthew was feeling; at his age

he hadn't yet learned how to climb down gracefully, without loss of face. He said, 'Tell me about this rallying. Costs money, I understand?'

'Yes, but there's big money in it if you win the major races. Though you'd need to be sponsored for that.'

'Did you know Nigel Fontenoy was going to leave you his share of the business?'

'He'd hinted, but it was blackmail, I didn't want his money! Not if it meant standing behind a bloody counter all my life, selling bits of old jewellery to people who've nothing better to do with their money.'

'The Fontenoys don't appear to have seen it like that. Certainly not old Mr Fontenoy.'

'Oh well, Uncle George! He's an expert, it's different for him – and it was for Nigel. They've been brought up to it.'

Mayo shifted his position. 'OK, then. Graham drove you home, then left you. Lindsay made you some black coffee. This was what time?'

'Lindsay says eleven. You'll just have to take her word for it. I wasn't looking at my watch at the time.'

'Don't get smart, lad! Then what?'

'Then nothing. I woke up next morning with the mother and father of a hangover, went to the shop and found it all locked up. I'd hardly got the door open before there was one of your lot on the doorstep telling me about Nigel.'

'You slept right through all the racket of that storm, in spite of the black coffee?' Carmody asked.

'Yes.'

The sergeant favoured Matthew with the steady, kindly look which yet had villains quaking, the one his own children would go to any lengths to avoid. 'I don't think you're telling me the truth, Matthew.'

Matthew shrugged, with a show of bravado just short of insolence. 'Think what you like. It's all the same to me.'

'There's the matter of Mr and Mrs Blamey swearing that they saw a car leaving your house again at ten past one. Your car.'

'How would they know it was my car? Old Blamey wouldn't recognize anything younger than a Ford Prefect.'

Mayo's way of dealing with cheeky young sprogs like Matthew was largely to ignore it. He was, Mayo was sure, a likeable enough lad in other circumstances, if immature for his age.

'I'll tell you what I think, Matthew. I think you weren't anywhere near as drunk as you made out. And the black coffee helped to sober you up even further. You knew your father had an appointment with Nigel that night and you waited until you heard him come home, then drove out yourself and killed Nigel Fontenoy.'

'You have to be joking!'

'No, I'm very serious indeed. We know that one of your father's pick-up trucks was used to transport Nigel Fontenoy's body from his shop to where it was dumped in Nailers' Yard. The way the weather was that night, the site must have been like a wet final at Twickenham. I think we shall have to examine what you were wearing. There must be some of the mud from the site clinging to your gear – and traces on your car.'

It was very quiet in the interview room. Outside, traffic ground up to the lights at the corner of Milford Road, inside, telephones rang, a door banged, the sound of raised voices could be heard. Deeley shifted his bulk on the hard chair and cleared his throat. Mayo waited, expecting Matthew to point out that mud wouldn't prove anything, he was on and off his father's building site all the time, but he didn't. He sat, very quiet and pale, looking down at the table. Eventually he said, 'I suppose I shall have to tell you what happened.'

A uniformed constable came in with mugs of tea requested half an hour ago and almost forgotten about, twice as welcome now.

'All right, lad,' Mayo began again when the tea had been dispensed, hoping the interruption hadn't given Matthew a chance to change his mind. 'Let's have it.'

'Where shall I start?'

'The Rose might be a good place.'

'All right. Well. All right, I'm not saying I didn't have more to drink than I should.' After an initial hesitation, he was away, anxious to get it off his chest. 'I'd had a bigger row than usual with my father and I wanted to get drunk, but I wasn't really as bad as everybody seemed to think. The owner – what's-his-name, Cellini – kept giving us funny looks, though, and in the end he asked us to leave, which we did.'

'And then?'

'Joss drove me home. I was sick in a flower bed when I got out of the car. The car lights woke Lindsay and when she heard all the kerfuffle she came across from the house to see what was happening. She helped me inside, made me some coffee and told me to get to bed, but I stayed where I was, on the sofa. I fell asleep, don't know for how long. Maybe it was my father's car coming in that woke me, I couldn't say, but anyway, it sounded like all hell was being let loose outside.'

'And?'

'Well, I realized after a minute or two that the storm had got up, and what a lot of damage it must be doing. For some reason, I started thinking about that old house and how easy it would be for the wind to blow it down – and I suppose that was only a step away from thinking how easy it would be to help it.'

'You thought knocking it down would solve all your dad's problems and you'd be the hero? Or was it that you thought he'd get the blame and you wanted to punish him?' Mayo asked.

'No!' Matthew protested. 'I don't know,' he amended, 'I don't remember what I thought! I don't believe I stopped to think very much at all. It just seemed like the most brilliant idea I'd ever had.'

'How did you get there?'

'My car, of course.'

'You were sober enough to drive?' But that was more of a reproof than a question. Mayo had seen enough drivers with a skinful to know how often the devil looks after his own.

'My car's acquired a dent or two that it didn't have before,' Matthew admitted, with a pale attempt at humour. 'Anyway, I made myself some more coffee and drove over to the building site, took the JCB across the road and well, that was it.'

'Come on, there's a bit more to it than that! How d'you get the JCB going, for one thing?'

'No problem, if you know how to hot-wire it. And the cab wasn't locked. It belongs to the contractors and they should immobilize the plant, leave things secure, but sometimes they don't bother. There's always rows about it.'

'So you got in and drove it, just like that?'

'It wasn't the first time I'd had a go! I've been mucking around on the site machinery since I was six years old.'

'All right, I believe you. So you drove it where?'

'I went to the old house, straight through the fence at the back, and clouted a couple of the props with the bucket. As soon as the second one went, the whole house sort of slid sideways and in about a minute it was total collapse. It was fantastic, I'd never have believed it if I hadn't seen it!'

Clearly, whatever remorse Matthew now felt, he didn't altogether regret the kick he'd got out of it at the time. Well, who'd never experienced that primitive satisfaction of knocking things down? A baby shoving a pile of coloured plastic building bricks over or bashing a spade on a sandcastle, a kid aiming a kick at a stack of tins in a supermarket? A steeplejack demolishing a mill chimney?

'You're a bloody young fool, you know that? Apart from anything else, you might have been killed. Don't you know that in the wrong hands, machines like that can be lethal?'

'I knew what I was doing,' Matt said sulkily.

'We've all heard that one, Matthew. So what did you do after that?'

'Nothing. Well, I took the JCB back and went home.'

'And all this without seeing a soul?'

Matthew hesitated. 'No, I didn't see anybody,' he said finally.

It was the only part of his story they didn't believe.

'This may be hard for you, Matthew, but are you absolutely sure you didn't see anybody?' Mayo asked.

'Yes, I'm sure.'

'Nobody at all?'

'I've said so, haven't I?'

Mayo sighed. 'Let's go over this last part again.'

But nothing would budge him.

By nine that evening, it was beginning to be apparent to Abigail that the law of diminishing returns was operating in a big way: the more work she put in, the less results she was obtaining. She rubbed her eyes, closed them and decided it was time to pack it in.

Everyone else had gone home on that floor, and Mayo saw her light shining through the opaque glass panels that separated her office from the corridor as he too left for home. He popped his head in.

'Still here, Abigail?' She jumped a mile, as guilty as if she hadn't been working thirteen hours with scarcely a break. 'Time you went home,' he said with a smile. But he sat down in the chair opposite, stretched his legs out and leaned back with his hands in his pockets.

'Matthew Wilding,' he said after a moment or two. 'It's bothering me. I don't see any reason for disbelieving him about knocking the house down – nobody would make up a daft story like that as an alibi, not Matthew, anyway – and if he did, and if that's what he was doing, and if Lindsay Hammond is telling the truth, it puts him out of the frame for the murder, but . . .'

'You still think he saw somebody?'

'I know he did. And I think it was probably his father – which is why he won't say. Understandable. He's told us the truth about the rest of what happened, which couldn't have been easy for him, and he's guilty as hell about his dad – guilty, or scared stiff.'

'Or it could be he's frightened because he saw someone he mistook for his father in the dark. Someone who looks like him.'

'Someone like Joss Graham, for instance?' Mayo rubbed his chin.

And then Abigail told him what she had thought after their meeting with Joss Graham on the building site, and later, after seeing Naomi Graham. He sat thinking it over for a while, then stood up. 'Tom Callaghan next, then. Well, tomorrow'll do, he won't be going anywhere. Time I was off home now. You, too.'

'I was just on my way.'

Abigail closed the Fontenoy file, shuffled together a pile of reports, left for yet another day the pile of official bumf she'd sworn to get through, and went home. Bed, and sleep, seemed infinitely attractive.

Home was the cold ashes of the previous night's fire, breakfast dishes in the sink, a film of dust on the furniture, a hastily constructed sandwich eaten before the electric fire. Her mother would not have been proud of her.

Eyes closing of their own volition in the warmth of the fire, she decided that domesticity wasn't her forte and wondered vaguely, yawning her way upstairs, whether she was even suited to living alone, recalling the casual orderliness of Ben Appleyard's flat the one time she'd been there, its purposefulness and self-sufficiency, its shelves and shelves of books – and the stack of papers beside the word processor.

Bed was a cold shiver because she'd forgotten to switch the electric blanket on. Later, when the duvet she'd wrapped tightly around herself made her too hot, she woke up sweating and couldn't get to sleep again, chasing insubstantial shadows. Apart from what she'd just been discussing with Mayo – what she was sure Naomi had been going to tell her – during that visit she knew she'd seen something else she'd subconsciously registered as important, though what it was remained as stubbornly elusive as the sleep that continued to evade her.

Callaghan was located by telephone the next morning, without too much difficulty, at the TV centre.

'No, no, don't you come here,' he replied hastily when this was suggested to him. 'I'll come over to you – or better still, why don't we meet halfway – at the golf club, say, where I'm a member? I'm sure you're as pushed for time as I am.'

He wasn't the man to neglect the opportunity of being seen, but in the circumstances Mayo thought it surprising that he'd suggested such a public meeting place, unless it was to demonstrate that he had nothing to fear from being seen in such suspect company.

He was waiting for them at the entrance to the clubhouse when they drew up, and came forward with hand outstretched, expansive as if they were welcome guests at his country house rather than police officers who might be there to give him a decidedly unpleasant half hour. He ordered coffee at the bar and then took them to a quiet corner by the picture windows where three armchairs were ranged round a low table, shielded from the rest of the room by a bank of climbing plants and overlooking a fairway and thickly wooded countryside beyond.

He talked pleasantries which Mayo let him carry on with until the coffee had been brought and poured and the waitress had disappeared. 'Mr Callaghan, we're not here on a social visit. Certain information has come to light since the last time we spoke to you that we need to talk to you about.'

With a practised gesture, Callaghan signalled him to go on, at ease in his chair with his famous smile pinned on, wearing a dark navy shirt buttoned to the neck, no tie, a light jacket almost the same silver as his blow-dried hair, beautifully cut navy slacks and pale grey moccasins.

When Mayo, well aware he was being brutal, but seeing no way out of it, brought up the subject of Callaghan's daughter, the smile barely slipped, but his face froze, as if the smile were painted on to a mask. 'I don't see,' he replied through stiff lips, 'what that has to do with Nigel Fontenoy's murder.'

'Let's not prevaricate, Mr Callaghan. I'm sorry to have to broach this subject, believe me, I've no wish to open old wounds, but I think you're aware that when your daughter died there was a certain amount of talk that she'd been involved with an older man.'

'If there was, nobody passed it on to me.'

Mayo said patiently, 'I suggest we shall finish with this much quicker if you're honest with us. Nigel Fontenoy was the name mentioned . . . and I've reason to believe you were well aware of this. If not at the time, as you say, then it's certainly something you've learned about during the last few weeks.'

'I find this exceedingly distasteful.'

'I'm sorry. But do you deny you met and talked with Sharon Wallace a few weeks ago? And that she gave you a bracelet which had belonged to your daughter? Which may have been given to her by Fontenoy?'

Two golfers came into view, looking like outsize children in their primary-coloured gear, dragging golfing trolleys behind them. Callaghan watched them walk the length of the fairway before he answered. Finally, he said, 'You've obviously talked to Sharon Wallace. Yes, she gave me the bracelet, and told me what Judy had said, that she'd asked her to keep it so that I wouldn't see it. I had to believe it was Nigel who gave it to her. Well, are you implying that I killed him, simply because of that?'

'No, I've no reason at this point to believe you had anything to do with his death.'

'I'm glad to hear it. Because in no way did I kill him. Not that I didn't think about it. Not that I haven't wished him dead every minute of my waking life since learning about him and Judy, but that's a very different thing from actually having the moral courage to make it happen. He took from me the one person who made my life worth living, after smirching a young and beautiful life, and I'm not ashamed to say I rejoice that he's dead. But I wasn't the instrument of his death, more's the pity.'

There was a silence after this. Mayo could find nothing to say because, though he couldn't condone, as a father he could find it in his heart to sympathize.

'I kept the bracelet Sharon gave me,' Callaghan went on. 'My first idea *was* to confront Nigel with it and then find some way of making him pay, perhaps kill him, who knows? But I couldn't do it, I was afraid that I mightn't have the guts when it came down to it. After I heard he was dead, I threw the bracelet in the river and that was the end of it.' He put his head in his hands, struggling for composure. He looked old and weary, his eyes empty, when he eventually raised his head. 'If you don't think I killed Nigel, what is it you want to talk about?'

'We need to know more about his background. You knew

him since you were at school together. You and Nigel Fontenoy and Jake Wilding.'

'Oh yes, we go back a long way, the three of us.'

'What do you know of Naomi Graham?' Mayo asked abruptly, and was rewarded by seeing a spark of sudden interest warming those cold eyes.

'Naomi? Jake's ex? I haven't seen her for nearly twenty years. Not since she left Jake in the lurch with young Matthew.'

'Did you know she was back in Lavenstock? With an older son she claims is Jake Wilding's?'

'That's what she's claiming, is it? Well, it's possible, but not true. If you've spoken to Naomi, you don't need me to tell you that she's apt to confuse fact with fiction. She says what suits her at the time. And yes, the child could've been Jake's, I'll grant you that. But he wasn't.'

'He's very like him.'

'Is he? Well, I haven't seen him, so I wouldn't know. But Jake's very like his Uncle George, come to that, yet that doesn't make George his father.'

It was true, Abigail thought, you could never predict when a family likeness would appear, or when it was likely to skip a generation. Nigel Fontenoy hadn't looked much like his father, George – the requisite genes seemed to have bypassed him and yet had been passed on through him to his son. Joss bore a passing similarity to Jake Wilding, yes, but Abigail had also glimpsed a fleeting yet far stronger resemblance to someone else – to a face, stiffened in death, but recognizably of the same cast of feature as Joss Graham's. 'It was Nigel Fontenoy who was Joss's father, wasn't it?'

'Yes, Inspector Moon, it was Nigel. Definitely. He told me so himself, at the time. To do him justice, he wanted to marry her, there was nothing he wanted more than a child, but she'd have none of it. Apparently, they'd quarrelled over something or other and presumably that was how she took her revenge.'

'Do you know what their quarrel was about?'

'No, but it was more than just a tiff. When I let Nigel know she was back in town he went quite pale. And before you ask, yes, I enjoyed telling him that, quite deliberately, hoping she'd make trouble for the bastard. I live in the knowledge that I might have succeeded.'

Mayo stood up. 'Thank you, Mr Callaghan, you've been very helpful.' His voice was without expression. Abigail slipped her notebook into her bag and also stood up.

'You're welcome,' Callaghan said bleakly.

23

When they returned from the golf club, Abigail found a note on her desk to say that Jermyn's had telephoned and she rang them back immediately.

Alec Macaudle's first words were an apology for the length of time it had taken him to return her call. He had been out of the country and had only just returned, he told her in a prissy, Morningside accent. He was deeply shocked at the news about Mr Fontenoy and was more than willing to help, insofar as he was able.

'Yes, indeed,' he answered her first question, 'I do recall my last meeting with him, poor man – very well. We lunched together and had a very fruitful discussion.' He was deeply regretful that all the long negotiations had come to naught. He had been looking forward to a long and pleasant association, he said, well launched into what Abigail feared was going to turn into a long-winded lament. 'Perhaps his heirs and assigns – ' he intimated.

Imagining Mr Macaudle as a pink little man with well-brushed grey hair and a pursy mouth, Abigail assured him that any inquiries the police were making would not interfere with any approaches Mr Macaudle might wish to make to Fontenoy's about their business deal, and then asked her second question, fully expecting to be met with further pomposity: had Mr Fontenoy, when they met, any other business to discuss with him? Such as, she suggested, requesting a second opinion on a valuable piece he had brought with him?

'Oh, you mean the Fabergé!'

Macaudle's response was immediate and unequivocal,

going straight to the point, causing Abigail to revise her opinion of his digressiveness, while at the same time the name Fabergé set a small, urgent bell ringing somewhere at the back of her mind.

'What a find!' he went on. 'Well, Mr Fontenoy himself had a good idea what it might be worth and that it was genuine, but he needed expert attribution, and knowing that I was an acknowledged authority on the subject,' he asserted modestly, 'he came to me before making a decision about it. I felt privileged to be able to help, and to say that in my opinion, the piece was genuine. You realize, of course, that many imitations of Fabergé objects have found their way on to the market during the course of the years, countless copies have been made. But this was the real thing. They're very rare, you know, these flowers, and with the wonderful provenance which he said existed – '

'Would you mind, Mr Macaudle,' Abigail intervened, 'describing this er – flower – to me?'

'When I say flower, you mustn't underestimate it, Inspector. I'm talking about a very fine work of art. But have you not seen it?' There was a pause. 'Oh dear, you're not saying that it's been – stolen?'

'I don't know. But it's not where it's supposed to be. That's why I should like a description of it, please.'

'Och,' Mr Macaudle said faintly, 'what times we live in!' Then, quickly recovering, he proceeded briskly, and with total recall, to describe the piece for her in minute detail. 'Well, a catalogue description might go something like this: "A sprig of honeysuckle in gold, three flowers and berries, the flowers enamelled, with white gold filament stamens. The leaves carved in dark green nephrite, the entwined stems in red gold, the berries in rhodonite. On one flower is poised a bee in black enamel, diamonds and rubies, on another an enamelled tortoiseshell butterfly. The spray is set in a columnar-shaped vase in green gold, engraved to represent tree bark, with a foliate border round the base in red gold studded with rose diamonds." '

'Goodness!'

'Yes, indeed, but even that gives no real indication of what it's really like. You'd have to see it to appreciate the inspired engraving, the tender pink and cream shading of the enamel on the petals, the way the stems twine down and around the vase – well, what I can only call the sheer artistry of the composition.' Slightly overcome by his own lyricism, the jeweller coughed and added prosaically, 'What's more, it actually bears the initials of the workmaster, the man who created it, which is unusual. H.W. Henrik Wigstrom.'

'Any indication of its worth?'

The lengthy silence at the other end made Abigail feel she'd unknowingly transgressed some code of ethics. Finally, Macaudle said severely, 'A hitherto unknown Fabergé piece? How can that possibly be evaluated? There are things of more importance than money.' Relenting, he added, 'All I can tell you is that these flowers are extremely rare, certainly one of this quality, and that if sold I would confidently expect it to reach well into six large figures. Especially, I may say, with the very special provenance this one has.'

'Which was?'

Another weighty pause. 'Well, of course, I didn't see it, but I understood from Mr Fontenoy that there exists a document – a letter, written in Russian – proving beyond doubt the piece was commissioned from Fabergé and intended as a twenty-first birthday gift in June, 1918 for the Grand Duchess Tatiana Romanov from her father, the Tsar of Russia. I'm afraid the poor young lady was destined never to receive it, since by then the whole family were prisoners in Ekaterinburg, where they were later shot by the revolutionaries.'

After a moment for this to sink in, Abigail asked, 'And how did the piece come to be in Mr Fontenoy's possession?'

'Never ask an antique dealer that! I certainly didn't. Many of these things came out of Russia after the terrible events of the revolution, by various means.'

'You mean they were stolen?'

'Oh, undoubtedly some of them were, with all the looting and so on that went on, but as far as this one goes, who can tell?'

'It was in some sort of box, I understand?'

After the minutely detailed description of the jewelled honeysuckle spray, she wasn't surprised to receive a similarly detailed one of its fitted case, of white polished holly wood, with the name of Fabergé, in the Russian alphabet, stamped on the satin lining of the lid.

'I must tell you,' Macaudle said before their conversation was ended, 'that I had reservations – not about the authenticity of the piece, to be sure, but about this letter Mr Fontenoy spoke of. One would need to see it and have it expertly assessed, but I understand there was some slight difficulty over that.'

'What sort of difficulty?'

'I believe it wasn't actually in his possession at the moment, but held by someone else.'

'I don't suppose he said who that was?'

'I fear not, though he seemed confident of producing it. Without it, needless to say, the flower would be worth considerably less.'

After Mayo had been acquainted with this latest development, looking somewhat deep in thought, he followed Abigail down to the incident room to put the rest of the team in the picture, or those who were not out of the office. Coffee cups were filled, cigarettes lit to add to the already thick fug of tobacco smoke in the room. Mayo perched on the table in front of the blackboard. 'Go ahead, Inspector Moon.'

They heard her out, and she saw their faces registering varying degrees of incredulity, amusement, suspicion. With some justification, she had to allow. Cases involving jewelled birthday presents from the Tsar of Russia to his daughter had not hitherto featured very prominently among the day to day break-ins, rapings, muggings, drunk and disorderlies and domestic violence that formed the rich pattern of ordinary life at Milford Road nick.

'No kidding!' said Deeley, when she'd eventually finished.

'You'd better believe it, Pete. It's true as I stand here.'

Later, after the buzz of excitement had died down and the room had gradually cleared to leave only Atkins and

Carmody – apart from one or two uniformed staff dealing with telephones and word processors – with Abigail and Mayo, Mayo said, 'At risk of stating the obvious, this establishes two things – that this Fabergé object was almost certainly connected to Fontenoy's murder, and that what Fontenoy wanted from Naomi Graham, via Jake Wilding, was the letter of provenance.'

From Atkins's pocket had come his familiar pouch and his pipe, which he now proceeded to fill and tamp down. Having finished packing it, he struck a match on the sole of his shoe, put flame to tobacco and from behind the ensuing pall of smoke, remarked, 'Using Wilding's gratitude for this alleged favour he owed him as a lever?'

Mayo walked to the window, threw it open and sat on the sill, arms folded. 'Right, George. Wilding hasn't seen fit to tell us what this favour was, but it must've been a sizeable one. One he isn't anxious to talk about, either.'

'Forde Manor,' Atkins stated, unmoved by the broad hint, inured to offence where his smoking was concerned.

'What?'

'Speaking from hearsay, mind, but there was a lot of talk last year when Wilding nipped in smartish and bought Forde Manor, just before Save All's announcement they were going to build a hypermarket. And Nigel Fontenoy was a member of the Chamber of Commerce, which might or might not mean anything . . . I'll say no more, and don't quote me.'

If Atkins, who knew more about Lavenstock than God, said so, it would be true. Mayo said, almost forgiving him his pipe, 'That's a better reason for Wilding agreeing to do what Nigel asked him than we've come up with so far, George, and one I'm inclined to believe. Right then, so we put him, and Matthew, on hold. It's possible that Matthew, for all he's denied it, knew about the Fabergé in the safe, and that his father did, too, for that matter, through Christine – but I think both are becoming long shots. Callaghan I think we can cross out. Leaving us with our latest suspect, Joss Graham. Who interests me very much. For whatever reason, he's deeply implicated in all this. It's quite possible he knew all about this Fabergé business and decided both objects would be better in his hands – if in fact the idea wasn't at his mother's instigation. Money like that would mean something to them.'

'Money isn't something that interests Naomi,' Abigail said.

'Money of that sort interests everybody,' Mayo averred.

'How come she had this letter in the first place?' asked Carmody.

'Maybe she lifted it when she worked for the Fontenoys, and that's what Fontenoy was so uptight about. According to Callaghan, they quarrelled over something or other just before she dropped out of the scene,' Abigail reminded him. 'But did Graham have to kill Fontenoy?'

'We don't know that he meant to go as far as that,' Mayo said, 'but who's to say, except him? I don't somehow feel the usual rules apply where Joss Graham's concerned. And there are deep undercurrents in all this. We need to have another session with him, immediately. At the moment, we're going too much on supposition.'

Yet no one knew better than he did that that was largely how it worked – putting forward a theory and then testing it out to see if it held water.

A telephone rang somewhere behind them. A WPC stood up and called out, 'There's someone at the front desk asking to see you, ma'am.'

'Sorry,' Abigail said. 'They'll have to wait, I'm busy.'

'She says to tell you her name's Lindsay Hammond, ma'am. It's urgent and she won't see anyone else.'

Abigail cursed silently but soon curbed her feelings of irritation at the interruption, realizing that Lindsay Hammond, of all people, wouldn't have come down to the station if what she had to say wasn't important. 'I'll be along to see her right away. Could you rustle us up some tea or coffee?'

Lindsay looked different in some unidentifiable way that was nothing to do with clothes or make-up, though she'd done something different to her hair and wore a neat blue suit that emphasized the colour of her eyes. Maybe it was the way she sat, not with her eyes lowered and knees and feet demurely together, but confidently, with her legs crossed.

192

She looked older. Nevertheless, she was finding it difficult to begin with what she had to say. Abigail helped her out.

'You're studying music, aren't you? Hasn't your term started yet?'

'I've been ill, glandular fever, it comes and goes. My tutor knows and in view of what's been happening . . . well, anyway, I needn't go back yet.' She drank some tea, wrapping her slender-fingered hands round the thick white official china, and said suddenly, 'No, that's just something I made up, to account for . . . I've been very depressed, and my mother worries about me. But she knows now that I – it's not true, about the glandular fever. Well, the truth is, I had an abortion.'

Abigail thought that explained a lot about Lindsay Hammond. Some girls might dismiss an abortion lightly, but not girls like her. 'That must've been rotten for you,' she said gently.

'It was dire.' The girl sipped more coffee, her eyes wide above the rim of the cup. 'But it's over. I wasn't the first and won't be the last, as they say.' Despite the flippant words, the pain, shame and despair were naked on her face, but then suddenly she smiled, a totally transforming smile that warmed and lit up her face and for a moment made her beautiful. It was her mother's smile and again Abigail noticed what lovely eyes she had, not the same blue-green as her mother's, but the same shape, grey with thick dark lashes. The illumination was as brief as it was beautiful. Then her face fell back into its habitual grave composure.

'Do you want to tell me who it was?' Abigail prompted, thinking my God, not Nigel Fontenoy again.

'Does that matter?' Lindsay asked quickly, defensively. 'It wasn't anyone you know. Oh, I see! You think that's what I came about – that it's got something to do with Nigel's murder. In a way, it has, though not directly, I think.'

'Why don't you tell me what you have to say and let me judge?'

'I'm sorry, I've never been very good at getting to the point,' Lindsay confessed. She hesitated, then quickly plunged her hand into the large shoulder bag she carried and brought out a flat cardboard box, which she pushed across the table.

When Abigail opened it, she saw an amethyst and diamond pendant, fastened on to a gold chain, the clasp of which was broken. 'This seems to be one of the items missing from the Cedar House,' she said, after a moment. 'Where did you get it, Lindsay?'

'It was sent to me – as a present. Then after Nigel was killed, this came, with a note asking me to keep it safe.' Out of the bag came a screw of tissue paper. Opened, a heavy gold ring was revealed, set with a lapis-lazuli seal. Abigail picked it up and held it near the light and saw the bearded, two-faced god, Janus.

She looked assessingly at the girl sitting opposite. 'You realize this is the ring Nigel Fontenoy was assumed to be wearing when he was killed?' Lindsay gave a barely perceptible nod. 'You know who sent them to you?'

Lindsay bit her lip. 'She helped me when I needed it . . . I was desperate and I hadn't a clue what to do, but she found out. She's only been in England a few months, and she's younger than me but she knows about things like that. I couldn't refuse to help her in return.'

'Who exactly are we talking about?' They had to be sure.

Lindsay swallowed. 'Cassie Andreas.'

Cassie. That dark, memorable face. That strong, butch girl. Everything that applied to her brother could equally apply to her.

Joss Graham walked very carefully down the narrow stairs and stood in the doorway of the little sitting room, watching his mother.

She knelt in front of the tin trunk which had stood in the middle of the room, half-packed, a nuisance to everybody, for days. Now it was almost empty, the contents strewn about the floor. He could see that wooden toolbox of hers, open, in the bottom of it. He sat on a chair arm and watched her as she pretended to tidy the already neatly assembled tools in the tray. It satisfied him deeply to see how nervous she was, that her hands trembled, that she was deliberately avoiding looking at him.

Finally, she put the tray on the floor, lifted up the false bottom and took out the leather pouch that he knew contained the gold bangle. 'I'm going to give this to Cassie,' she said, holding up the bangle so that it gleamed in the light. 'I've no use for it any more. D'you think she'll like it? It's quite pretty.'

He ignored the bright bauble. 'How did you know where they were hidden?' he asked conversationally.

She turned even paler than she'd been before, but he was glad to see that she wasn't going to make a pretence of not understanding that he meant the Fabergé flower, and the letter, because that sort of thing was liable to annoy him. And he was already angrier than he'd ever been in his life, except once, on that memorable day when Nigel had made the twin mistakes of disowning him, and showing them the flower.

'I just kept on looking until I did find them,' Naomi said. 'Under the floorboards was a fairly obvious place, anyway — and they're easy enough to pull up, God knows, with most of them rotten.'

'What made you think they were here at all, in this house?'

She raised her eyes to his, still kneeling on the floor, and he saw that the fear had left her. She looked sad and careworn in the dusty, tatty old black she was wearing, like an old Greek widow. 'Oh Joss, when I heard Nigel Fontenoy had been murdered and found that the letter had disappeared, there was nothing else I *could* think. What have you done, you and Cassie? What made you do it?'

He said harshly, 'The bastard deserved it.' And as he said it, he saw the scenes which had led up to Fontenoy's murder in fast-action replay: first, the night in the garden when she had told him he was not Jake Wilding's son, but Nigel Fontenoy's. And next, what had happened on the following day.

It had been Cassie's idea to go and see Nigel.

Joss's first thought had been to quit Lavenstock, to get away, forget the whole thing. Then he'd begun to agree with

Cassie, why should he leave empty-handed? Nigel Fontenoy wasn't rolling in it, but he wasn't exactly on the breadline.

Cassie went with him. They had simply walked into the shop, found Nigel alone, and told him who they were and what they'd come for: Joss demanded either recognition as his son, or enough money to make it worth his while to go away. At first disbelieving, Nigel had eventually lost his temper and said contemptuously that he would never in a million years get anything from him, what proof was there that Joss was his son?

'Because my mother says so,' Joss had replied.

'Oh? And how would she know? How many other candidates d'you think there were?'

Joss's temper was slow to catch fire, but unquenchable once it did. He had nearly put his hands round Nigel's throat then and there, in the shop, in broad daylight, strangled the life out of him and knocked the supercilious smile from his face for ever. But something inside him said no, wait. The bugger deserved to die, but not before he, Joss, had found some way to benefit from it.

The possibility opened up even before they left the shop. They'd prepared to leave then, suddenly, Nigel's attitude had changed. 'You do something for me,' he'd said, 'and I'll make it worth your while.' He went on to tell them about the Russian letter, which he swore Naomi had stolen from him, and had even shown them the Fabergé flower to add authenticity to his story when they looked dubious. If Joss could get the letter from his mother, he would not find Nigel ungenerous. 'And to show I'm in earnest,' he'd added, 'take this, it's worth a bob or two.' And he'd tossed to Cassie an amethyst and diamond pendant that was lying on his desk, waiting, with one or two more things, to be picked up by the man who did his repairs. 'It only needs a new clasp.'

After a few minutes' silence, Joss had promised, with apparent docility, that he would do his best to get the letter.

Nigel was looking very pleased with himself as they left. No doubt he thought he'd made a good bargain, but then, he didn't know Joss. Joss had been absolutely livid. A mouldy old pendant that didn't even fasten properly, like throwing a bone to a dog! And giving it to *Cassie*! Cassie, who despised wearing any kind of jewellery. It was another thing to add to the list of what he'd make Nigel Fontenoy pay for.

Just how wasn't clear, but bigger obstacles than this hadn't stopped Joss before. He'd never admitted to being thwarted by anything, whatever he'd ever wanted to do in his life, and he wasn't about to start now. He began to brood on how he could get even.

Once back home, they'd searched for the letter, and found it under the false bottom of Naomi's toolbox, an obvious place, where she had always kept such treasures as she had, like the gold snake bangle.

The letter had not, however, been taken to Nigel as promised, because long before then, Joss and Cassie had begun to talk of getting the Fabergé for themselves as well.

'Why did you do it?' Naomi's voice rose to a despairing wail. 'Why did you have to kill him? He *was* your father, after all.'

'What has that got to do with anything? He was your lover once, but he was prepared to cheat you out of what was yours. He wouldn't acknowledge me as his son, but he was prepared to use me, to buy me off if I'd get that letter for him. It was his own fault. I wouldn't have killed him if he'd done what I asked.'

She closed her eyes, then, gripping the edge of the trunk for support, got to her feet.

'Don't waste any more of my time,' he said through his teeth. 'I want to know what you've done with them – the flower and the letter.'

'They're where you'll never get at them,' she said. 'I've put them in safe hands.'

'I thought you might've been stupid enough to do something like that.' She was really a very stupid woman, his mother. Useless. If she'd played her cards properly, she could've had anything she wanted. As it was, she deserved everything that had ever happened to her, just as Fontenoy had. He felt power surge in him as he swooped to the toolbox. Hardly knowing how it had got there, he was aware of the smooth, remembered feel of the wooden cap of the needle-sharp engraving tool in his palm.

She grabbed his wrist with bony fingers that were surprisingly strong and tried to force the burin away. They struggled, swaying to and fro. He couldn't hear her, under the din of the train rushing through the cutting, but he could see her, her face contorted in a parody of that painting called 'The Scream'. He hadn't heard the roar of Cassie's motorbike, either, had no idea she'd come in until he saw her standing in the doorway.

As when Abigail had called at the ramshackle brick house before, there was no response when she knocked. This time she tried the door.

It wasn't locked. The knob turned and she stepped inside to a scene that would remain with her for the rest of her life. Nothing she had yet encountered had prepared her for this. Her hand went to her mouth. The gorge rose in her throat, she felt sick. She backed away and knocked into Carmody, a couple of steps behind her. She took several deep breaths, reminded herself that she was trained and able to cope with this, and forced herself to look again.

'Hell's bells,' Carmody said.

Blood everywhere. Three bodies.

Naomi Graham was lying on the floor, grey hair fanned half over her face, with what looked like one of her own engraving tools driven into her chest. Her son was lying beside her in a pool of blackening blood, a small, sharp chisel on the floor beside him. Cassie slumped in a chair, eyes closed. The room stank like a slaughterhouse.

Cassie's eyes opened. Slowly, as if they were being forced to against her will.

So there were only two dead bodies. And one severely shocked girl, alive but in a near-catatonic state. Only one dead body, it soon emerged, since Joss Graham was also still alive, though only just.

24

At the Cedar House, the lamps were lit and a small coal fire smouldered in the hearth. It was a mild day, though dark and heavy.

'You're my second visitors today. Christine's just been here. We were talking about reopening.' Frail and slightly tottery, George Fontenoy bent dangerously forward to attack the sullen coals, finally succeeding in coaxing the fire to spring into flame.

'You are keeping the business going, then?' Abigail asked.

'I couldn't cope with it alone, but I've spoken to Christine and she's more than willing to come back and run the shop for me, with a view to an eventual partnership. I intend to buy Matthew out – the share of the business my son left to him. As you've probably gathered, he lacks any attachment to it.' George watched the flames and smoke leap up the chimney; if he was disappointed, he'd clearly no intention of letting it show.

'Pity he's not interested,' Mayo said.

'From my point of view, yes, but not from Matthew's. He's come to his senses and is doing what he should've been doing all along, working with his father. I'm not speaking of any obligations to Jake, it's simply right for Matthew. He'll make a success of it, you'll see. He's very like his father. But that isn't why I asked you to come here. I would have been in touch with you before, but –' He hesitated. 'Are you at liberty to tell me about – about what happened, Chief Inspector?'

'If it won't upset you too much.'

'That doesn't matter. I'd rather know.'

Mayo couldn't even begin to imagine how it would feel at George's age to discover you had a grandson you'd never known to exist, then to find out he'd killed your son, his own father. It was an insupportable situation which must already have placed obligations and burdens on him he didn't need. Yet he'd a right to know what had happened, to have the chance to come to terms with it. Swiftly, Mayo gave him what facts he ought to know. What seemed to puzzle the old man most was how Joss Graham had got into the shop that night.

'Nigel let him in because he was told Joss now had the provenance he wanted, although he must've been surprised. It'd been several weeks since he'd put the idea to Joss and nothing had transpired, so presumably he'd thought the deal was off. Time was running out, Naomi was on the point of leaving Lavenstock, and that, I suppose, was why he'd pressured Jake Wilding into trying to get the letter for him.'

What Mayo didn't say was how much the randomness of the whole thing had struck him – that the circumstances of Fontenoy's death had seemed almost accidental, that Joss Graham had planned only as a notional concept, trusting mostly to luck. It was the sort of single-minded, blinkered approach to any crime, the criminal's unquestioning belief in the success of his actions, the reckless disregard for the usual cover-ups, that put the fear of God into Mayo whenever he encountered it, because no amount of applied logic could make any sense out of a plan which had never existed in the first place.

'So he simply walked in, killed my son, and took the Fabergé from the safe with Nigel's own keys.' Only a slight tremble in George's voice betrayed his feelings.

'That's how he said it was, and his sister corroborates his story.'

'Ah yes, the girl. Naomi's daughter.'

'Cassie wasn't involved in the actual murder. The whole thing was, to begin with, a sort of *folie à deux*, and it's very possible she was the moving spirit. She's capable of it – but in the end, Joss went too far, even for her. Her relationship with her mother, not to say her brother, was complex. Naomi

200

genuinely didn't care what her children did, Cassie desperately tried to make her care. She went out of her way to be outrageous, pretended that her mother meant nothing to her, but when it came to it, and she saw Joss stab Naomi, it was too much.'

Cassie – proud, fierce Cassie – in deep shock after what had happened, had initially been put into a hospital bed and heavily sedated, afterwards turning her face away and refusing to speak, except to ask how Joss was.

'Still in intensive care,' Abigail had told her. 'Early days yet, but they believe there's at least a chance he'll pull through.'

'My mother won't.'

'I'm sorry.' And Abigail had found that one small part of her was. There'd been something about Naomi, a free spirit who'd lived by her own principles, such as they were. She'd been a disaster as a mother, yet Cassie at least had loved her, certainly more than she'd known, and nothing Naomi had done could have justified her terrible end.

During the days that followed, one police officer or another had been constantly at Joss's side. There were times when he talked feverishly, times when he fell silent, times when he was forbidden by the doctors to speak at all. Then, after a while, Cassie consented to unburden herself, at first to nobody except Lindsay, although she made no objections about the WPC with a tape machine who sat to one side.

'What a bloody shambles,' Mayo had said, receiving these reports from Abigail.

'Yes, sir,' she'd answered stiffly.

He gave her a sharp glance. 'No blame attached to anyone. We couldn't have foreseen and avoided what happened.'

But she knew that she'd seen the weapon which had killed Naomi, days before Joss had killed his mother. 'It was the same weapon he used to kill Fontenoy. I knew it as soon as I saw it in her chest. It was what she called a burin – an engraving tool – which I'd seen the first time I visited her. I should've known then that it was the same weapon that had killed Fontenoy, it exactly fitted the description of the profile Timpson-Ludgate gave. I ought to have realized.'

'Well, you didn't. And we can all be wise after the event,'

Mayo said astringently, with scant sympathy. Sympathy was not what was needed here. The investigation which ended clean and sanitized and all wrapped up, where you didn't blame yourself for something or other, had yet to happen.

'Well,' George said with a sigh, 'I suppose you're wanting to see the Fabergé piece.'

They were indeed. When the flower hadn't turned up in a search of the house, when it had been clear that it, and the letter, had been the source of the row between Joss and his mother, it had been on the cards they'd been returned to George Fontenoy, even before he rang to say that he had them and wanted to offer some explanation.

'She brought them herself, you know . . . Naomi, that is, someone I'd never expected to see again, I must confess. The last time I'd seen her she'd been Jake's wife, Matthew's mother, before she went off like a gipsy with some Greek waiter, leaving Jake and little Matthew behind without a thought, poor little devil.' He stopped, embarrassed. 'I'm sorry, she's dead now. That was unpardonable.'

'She brought you the flower, and the letter?' Abigail prompted.

'They were hers, they both belonged to her by rights, you know.' He stood up now and, crossing the room to a wall safe hidden behind a picture, brought back a box of creamy white wood with tiny gilt hinges and clasps, which he deposited on a low table before the fire.

The honeysuckle spray which Alec Macaudle had so lyrically and accurately described lay on black velvet. George lifted it carefully and set it on the table. It was smaller than Abigail had imagined, not more than six or seven inches high, a lovely, gleaming thing of enamelled gold and precious stones. She began to understand the appeal of its restrained elegance and beauty. She wanted to touch, to examine the intricate detail, marvel at the exquisite workmanship.

Mayo thought, Christ, six figures?

'She brought the letter, too.' From inside the lid of the box, which it just fitted, George lifted and carefully unfolded a piece of yellowed paper, brittle on the creases, crossed with faded Cyrillic script. 'Afraid I can't decipher it for you, it's in

Russian, which Tsar Nicholas and his children always used between themselves. Natural enough, I'd have thought, seeing it was their native language, but apparently anyone who was anybody at the court spoke French. I've been told, and there's no reason to think otherwise, that it's a birthday message to the Grand Duchess Tatiana, from her father.'

George passed a large manila envelope to Mayo. 'Think you'd better read this, too, it'll tell you more than I can. She had it all written out before she came, so there can be no more misunderstandings in future. May I make you some tea while you read it?'

Remembering the last occasion they'd drunk George's tea, and knowing Mayo's detestation of anything other than strong Indian, Abigail thought it might be kinder to everyone to decline but, feeling George was probably anxious to occupy himself while they read through the thick sheaf of lined foolscap Mayo was now drawing from the envelope, she said, 'Thank you, that would be kind.'

The sheets were covered with large, black, decorative-looking handwriting, the lines double spaced. Mayo flicked through them, then began to read carefully, passing each page to her as he finished.

The first one was headed: *This is a true account of how I came to be the rightful owner of a work of art in the form of a spray of honeysuckle, made in the workshops of Carl Fabergé and left to me by my dear aunt and godmother, Lilian Courtenay. I will try and describe, as she told it to me, how it came into her possession and what happened to it later.*

The account which followed began with the story of Naomi's aunt, a pretty and fun-loving ex-chorus girl who, in her late twenties and approaching the hump as far as her dancing days were concerned, had accepted the marriage proposal of a comfortably-off widower called William Charlton, who'd been an occasional lover of hers, in fact, for some time before his wife died. Giving up her stage career without too many pangs, she went off to live comfortably with him in his house in Streatham, until suddenly he died, leaving her in something of a quandary: according to the lawyers, his business had for some time been gently sliding downhill, and would have ended in bankruptcy sooner or later. As it was, Lilian was left with a pile of debts which she was fortunately able to pay off with insurances and the sale of the business, a wardrobe full of fashionable clothes, the house in Streatham and no income. Always resourceful, she changed her home into a boarding house, finding she could accommodate two or three lodgers at a time, mostly short-term lettings to theatricals.

Occasionally, she had people who stayed longer. One of these was an old man, a Russian émigré called Anton Svetskov, who arrived in London, via Austria, just before the war. He stayed with her for two years, his money slowly running out, growing more and more doddery, talking constantly about St Petersburg and the Imperial court, where he'd been a minor official, full of stories of his connections with the Romanovs, of their great palaces and their untold wealth, of how they spent money like water while the Russian peasants starved.

She took these stories with a pinch of salt, but she was sorry for the old fellow and let him talk. She would invite him into her sitting room to hear her play and sing, and he taught her to make Russian tea. The day inevitably came when he couldn't pay his rent, but she let him stay on out of the kindness of her heart. He ate nothing much, and after all, his room was a tiny boxroom: he was very little trouble.

Svetskov died in the same month the war started. When she was clearing out his room, Lilian found a trunk of rather dreadful old clothes, fit only for burning, some sepia photographs which meant nothing to her, and an ivory-coloured box.

The old humbug! was her first thought when she opened it. Here she'd been, keeping the old man, knowing him to be sad and lonely, thinking him penniless, when all the time he'd been sitting on this obviously extremely valuable object! Had he simply forgotten he had it? It was possible, it had been buried at the bottom of the trunk under those old clothes, and he'd been almost senile when he died. Or had he meant her to have it, for what she'd done for him? After all, she'd kept him and been kind to him, without any thought or hope of repayment, and he didn't have one single friend or relative that she knew of to leave anything to. In the circumstances, she'd no compunction about keeping the Fabergé for herself. It had 'ФАБЕРЖЕ' stamped in the white satin lining of the lid, which Svetskov had told her was 'Fabergé' in the Cyrillic script; she'd had to listen to more stories from Svetskov about the fabulous jewelled eggs and other Fabergé artefacts than she could remember.

She'd realized immediately that the flower must be worth a lot of money, especially when she'd had the letter that was also inside the box translated, which meant that maybe the old man's stories of his illustrious connections hadn't all been figments of his imagination, but she'd no idea how much it was really worth.

During the years that followed, she would look at it and tell herself that she was a fool to leave it lying there, but she couldn't bring herself to sell it. There was something that stopped her, something about its tragic history, and some fear of bad luck if she profited from it. Svetskov, for all his talk, had been a nobody at the court, he couldn't have come by it honestly, it must have been looted. Like many theatrical people, she was very superstitious. If she'd been in need of money, it might have been a different story, but she'd always made a comfortable living from her lodgers. She kept the flower until she was in her mid-sixties and dying of cancer, when she sent for Naomi, who was young, very hard up, and who wouldn't, she thought, have the same feelings about the piece that she had. She gave it to her, relating its history and advising her to sell it for what she could get.

Naomi had felt no better about the object than her aunt had done. *I couldn't have sold it and profited by it, either*, she wrote. *I didn't want to keep it, but I didn't know what else to do. Just at that time, for various reasons, I packed in my design course in Birmingham and went back to live and work at home in Lavenstock, selling my pieces wherever I could, mostly to George Fontenoy and his son, Nigel. Eventually, Nigel and I became lovers, and I told him about the Fabergé flower, which he offered to keep in his safe. I suppose I was very naive, letting him do that, but not so naive as to trust him with the Tsar's letter, as well.*

Abigail, hearing George at the door, sprang up to take the tray from him. He let her pour the weak liquid and hand out the thin, delicate cups and signalled to her to carry on reading when she'd done so, while he sat back and sipped his tea and waited for them to finish.

When Nigel discovered I was pregnant he wanted to marry me, Abigail read. *But I had all my life in front of me, I couldn't bear the thought of being tied down, and having to live in Lavenstock forever. In the end, I told him I was leaving, and that I wanted my Fabergé flower back. We had a bitter quarrel but he refused to give it up, so I had no choice but to leave it. How could I ever have proved it was mine, without expensive litigation? And anyway, part of me was glad to be rid of it, the money didn't matter. I had a strong feeling that the flower brought bad luck. I told Nigel he was welcome to it, it was his as far as I was concerned, and much good may it do him.*

It was all rubbish, Abigail was about to say, that sort of superstitious nonsense, when she looked up and caught George's expression. 'Read the last page,' he told her. Mayo, having already finished, passed it to Abigail and lifted his teacup, the contents of which were now cool enough to allow him to drink deeply, disposing of it without offence to their host, while Abigail read to the end of the long screed, right up to Naomi's large, scrawled signature.

'You'll notice she's given me permission to do as I wish with it,' George said, 'perhaps sell it and give the proceeds to charity. She seems to have thought that doing so might break its influence, and perhaps it will. Taking these things lightly is apt to rebound. Beautiful work of art though it is, it has a tainted history. It's brought nothing but grief and sorrow to everybody concerned with it.' A little French clock on the mantel busily measured off the seconds and a puff of gas blew from a lump of coal. 'She wasn't being fair. His reasons weren't entirely mercenary. He was a perfectionist, Nigel, I daresay he couldn't bear to think of that lovely thing only half complete without its true history. He was never in a position where he needed to sell it, so he hung on to it in the hope that some day Naomi would let him have the letter.'

Mayo felt it would be invidious to point out that the flower had never been Nigel's to part with. If he'd done so, would both he and Naomi have escaped being the last links in the long line of chance happenings, the randomness of fate which had finally landed on them as victims?

When they left, George came to the door with them, opening it on to the desolation of the garden. The great cedar had gone, and the smaller trees which had come down with it, but the rhododendrons were still flat and the whole garden was carpeted with a debris of small branches, twigs and round, scented cones, filling the air with a resiny tang.

'What a mess!' George looked at the dereliction, more bewildered by it than by anything that had happened. Then his brow cleared. 'Christine will have it seen to. What would we all do without Christine?'

Mayo put his key in the ignition. The traffic was heavy. Friday, people speeding home to spend the weekend with their loved ones. 'What are you doing this weekend, Abigail?'

She pulled a face. 'I'd better tackle some of the dust that's accumulated at home! And get some fresh air – there's a hill behind the cottage I haven't yet climbed.' And she smiled, a small, inward-turning smile with a hint of radiance, just for herself – and surely the man who could make her look like that? 'And you, sir?'

'Me?' Stabbed with an absurd jealousy, Mayo shrugged. 'I don't know.' Then, suddenly, he did. There was the letter from Alex, resting even now in his breast pocket, a talisman lying next to his heart. Like a schoolboy with his first love letter, he'd read and reread it, until it was already frayed on the creases. She was driving home with Lois on Wednesday. And maybe, his hopeful heart said, home would mean his home, at last, for both of them – his flat, 21a, Camberley Street. She'd be there always, they'd never disagree again, she'd be waiting for him every time he got home. Hallelujah!

The sheer lunacy of such thoughts pulled him up short. The vision of Alex as some idealized wife in an apron, a hot meal simmering in the oven, her career on the back burner . . . He came to earth, and laughed.

He knew suddenly that he'd never had any intention of

waiting until Wednesday. He looked at his watch. There'd be a lot to do – the flat to make respectable before his fastidious young woman arrived – his clocks would need their weekly winding, otherwise they'd all run down and be out of synch and throw temper tantrums like prima donnas. And after that, there was a long drive before him. He'd better get a move on.